A Scottish Comp

SINS AND SCANDALS
BOOK THREE

LAUREN SMITH

Lauren SMITH
TIMELESS ROMANCE

Copyright page

Cover design Holly Perret

The publisher is not responsible for websites (or their content) that are not owned by the publisher.

ISBN 978-1-958196-92-2 (ebook)

ISBN 978-1-947206-18-2 (print)

Chapter One

England, October 1911

Rowena Pepperwirth dashed along the lawn of the winter-browned grass of the Hampton House gardens. A gust of wind wrenched her hat from her head but she didn't stop running to chase it. Terror gripped her heart and blood pounded a violent tempo in her ears.

There was only one thing that mattered. A little girl in a blue dress and white pinafore, who could not be older than three, was climbing onto a stone fountain edge about fifty feet away. A fountain Rowena had seen up close only yesterday and which she knew with dreaded certainty had a very slick ledge…The icy water inside was thickly dotted with lily pads. If the child fell, she could drown as she scrambled to get free of the watery vegetation.

A distant roar filled her ears and her palms slickened with sweat as she raced down the garden path.

Please don't fall, please...She prayed she could reach the little girl in time. The distance between her and the fountain seemed infinite. The child could die if she wasn't fast enough...

Leaning forward, Rowena pushed her legs until they burned as she sprinted toward the child. She slid straight into the stone base, her knees smarting from the impact, but she ignored it while she grasped the girl by the back of her dress.

The surge of fear didn't fade immediately. Hands shaking, Rowena was immobile, holding the child above the water for a second before she recovered from the shock.

The little girl bounced and squealed, clapping her chubby little hands and peering into the fountain.

She was safe.

Rowena tugged her back into her arms, wrapping herself around the child protectively. Her hands shook and she had trouble breathing. It was all right. She'd gotten there in time. Shutting her eyes, she held the girl close, never more thankful she was fast on her feet.

"Fishes!" The little girl jabbed a delicate little finger at the water.

Rowena smiled and nuzzled the girl's cheek before kissing her. "Indeed, there are fish when it's warmer, but we mustn't catch them. You might fall in and then what would happen to you?" She feathered her fingers through the girl's curls, marveling at the way the light played upon strands as perfect as spun gold.

"No fishes?" the child queried solemnly, looking now at Rowena in a knowing way.

"No fishes."

"Thank 'eavens, miss!" A middle-aged nurse trundled round the corner of the nearest hedgerow, her face red and her breath uneven as she struggled to speak. "Wee bairn escaped me, she did." The woman's Scottish accent caught Rowena by surprise. Scots were common enough in London but in the countryside they were rare. She'd known that one of the guests at the Earl of Hampton's house party was Scottish, but she hadn't realized he'd brought a nurse with him or that he had a child. Then again, mentioning one's children in the midst of a house party wasn't done. Babes stayed in the distant nurseries, which saddened Rowena. She adored children. One of her dearest dreams was to have a brood of children running about her house someday.

"It's quite all right. I have her. She's safe." Rowena curled an arm around the child's waist, smiling as the little girl bounced excitedly and pointed at the few solitary fish that had so far survived the increasingly cold weather. Their sleek silver bodies ducked and dove in the murky depths of the fountain, and she watched them in fascination and single-minded determination.

"Papa!" the babe pronounced excitedly, and jabbed a little index finger toward the house.

"Is your papa here, little one? I'm sure he'd be worried to know you ran off without him. Fathers worry about their daughters. You must take care not to frighten him." The child's eyes, a soft dove gray, fixed on Rowena as though considering seriously what she'd said, and then she dropped onto her bottom on Rowena's lap, content to simply watch.

The nurse eased down onto the lip of the fountain base beside them, her face still flushed. "The wee one has fast legs, just like her father did when he was a bairn. Could never catch that child." The nurse's face was gentle with tenderness as she said this.

"Is she Lord Forres's child?" Rowena queried.

It had to be the man she'd met at dinner the previous night. The quiet, well-spoken, and all-too-handsome Earl of Forres had been the object of quite a few stolen glances from the ladies over the various courses at dinner. Rowena, only eighteen, was certain it wasn't proper for so many women to be sneaking looks at a man far down the table from them. But as this was her first official house party since her come-out in London a few weeks before, she wasn't quite sure if the social rules were different between London and the country. Naturally that meant she'd been glancing at him too. It was impossible not to. He was incredibly handsome, with intense eyes and a soft smile that did strange things to her body whenever he'd met her gaze. And the way he moved—in that graceful yet powerful way—had drawn every female eye to him over and over again.

"Aye, she's his all right." The nurse chucked the little girl under the chin and the child giggled.

Rowena held her breath as she stared down at the girl. She shared her father's serious gray eyes, but her light blond hair was a contrast to her father's dark brown locks. Did she take after her mother, then? Rowena didn't know much of Forres except that he was twenty-eight and well in-laid when it came to property and money.

That did not matter so much to her. Rowena's family was well off and titled, so she had no need to look for a wealthy husband. This left her free to enjoy meeting someone she would like to marry. She focused on the men themselves and not the social positions she could gain. She wanted to be viewed equally, as a partner, not a subordinate. Unlike her sister Milly, who dreaded the idea of marriage, Rowena looked forward to the challenges of sharing a life with someone and raising children, but she knew she had to choose the right person. Someone who would see her value and trust her to bring something to their marriage besides simply childbearing abilities.

That was why Forres had intrigued her the previous

evening. When he spoke, his rich, dark voice had an enticing Scottish lilt that seemed to curl in the air like a slow, dancing plume of smoke, mesmerizing her. The candlelight had illuminated his eyes and she hadn't been able to look away as he talked. His opinions on politics and social issues were well informed and he approved of women being equal to men. He was neither proud nor so opinionated as to alienate anyone during polite conversation. Even Milly, Rowena's older headstrong sister, had been impressed with Forres.

"I didn't know Lord Forres had a child. I thought he was unmarried."

There certainly hadn't been a wedding band on his finger. Little whispers had traveled down the table, escaping from behind the edges of water goblets as the ladies had passed along their observations to each other. The fact that he wasn't married had provoked quite the discussion among the women after the men had gone off to smoke cigars and drink. She'd taken to looking at him, and more than once his eyes had touched upon hers, making her feel dizzy. There was something about him, the curve of his lips in a hint of a smile, the intensity of his gray eyes as he watched her. It had made her body flush with heat.

"Aye, he's only got the one. Our countess passed a year ago and my lord's been sore for missing her." The older woman's face was somber as she spoke, and for a moment she was quiet. But then a little smile crept back onto her lips. "But now he's wife hunting." The nurse winked at her conspiratorially.

Wife hunting? She could just picture the darkly handsome earl prowling through the underbrush, rifle at the ready to hunt ladies who fluttered in autumn-colored gowns like a dozen pheasants. The image was silly enough to make her bite her lip to hide her smile. But then she focused on what the nurse had said. Forres *had* been married. His wife had died.

Rowena cuddled the excited child closer in her arms as she realized the little babe had no mother. All children should know a mother's love. She squeezed the girl in a hug. Rather than squawk as other children might, the little girl ceased her bouncing and settled more firmly in Rowena's lap. It felt...right in a way Rowena couldn't explain, and her longing for children of her own grew even stronger.

"She likes you. Blair doesn't like most women and hasn't had a chance to be around too many besides myself and the staff." The nurse was smiling widely now, a glimmer of hope in her eyes that Rowena didn't understand.

"Blair?" Rowena said, and the little girl lifted her head to stare back.

"That's me!" The child beamed at her.

"Nice to meet you, Blair." Rowena smiled back, then

turned her attention to the nurse. "He's wife hunting here in England? Why not take a bride closer to home?"

"I suppose," the nurse mused, "he doesn't want someone that reminds him of the previous Lady Forres. He doesn't share much of his heart; he's quiet, but a good man. He needs his heart healed. A good woman would do well for him."

Rowena brushed her fingertips over the curls by Blair's cheeks, tousling them. They were as soft as silk and as fine as a baby bird's feathers. She pondered over the nurse's speculations. Lord Forres was hunting for a wife to heal his broken heart? Her own heart twinged in pain at thinking of how lonely he must be. He sounded like a man who loved deeply. Rowena couldn't help but feel drawn to him now, knowing he bore such pain. It was rather romantic, in a sad way.

Before she could speak again, a man burst around the hedgerows, sprinting toward them. It was Lord Forres. His dark hair was in wild tangles about his head as though he'd dragged his hands through the strands, and his lips were peeled back in an almost feral snarl.

He skidded to a halt just a few feet away when he spotted the nurse first.

"Mrs. Finch!" he bellowed at the nurse. "Where the devil have you been? I've searched the entire house for you and Blair..." As he stared at his child, safe in Rowena's arms, the wild look in his eyes softened slightly.

"She's safe, my lord," Rowena said as she stood, tucking Blair against her right hip.

"Papa!" The little cherub smacked her hands together, wriggling in Rowen's hold.

"Oh, my wee heart." The earl strode over to Rowena and plucked Blair out of her arms before she could even protest.

Blair's cheeks pinkened and her little lips quivered when she seemed to notice her father's distress.

"There, there," Forres shushed the babe.

"She's fine, truly. I was able to catch her before she fell in," Rowena assured him.

"Fell in?" Clear eyes, gray as a winter's sky, met hers. A tremor rippled through her. How had she forgotten what looking at him made her feel? Dizzy, excited, and a little anxious. Of course, last night they'd had a dozen people between them, and all manner of candles, dishes, and other things to block them from speaking directly. Yet there had been one moment, when he'd joined in the toasting for the evening and he'd raised his glass. His eyes had traveled from face to face, lingering only on hers.

"Yes, she was climbing onto the edge of the fountain when I found her."

"Good God," he muttered. "I only knew she'd wandered away from the nursery." He gave Blair a kiss on her forehead before looking toward Rowena.

He combed his fingers through hair that was a little too

long for the current fashion. There was something different about him, as though the suit he wore was a costume. With his broad shoulders, great height, and muscled form, he was more fit for the role of a Scottish warrior of old than a gentleman in a garden. The thought of him in a kilt, brandishing a sword, like a man out of her deepest, secret dreams... another shiver rippled through her and she swallowed hard. She was still young enough to have silly daydreams about handsome lords whisking her away to castles.

"Thank you, Miss Rowena. I apologize for my...harsh reaction." Forres gripped little Blair's head gently with one strong hand as he clutched his daughter to his chest. He closed his eyes and nuzzled her soft curls.

"No need to apologize," Rowena said. She smoothed out her skirts, feeling a little embarrassed at witnessing such a strong show of emotion from a man who the nurse had said guarded his heart.

Forres met her gaze. "I went to check on Blair and when she was gone, I panicked...A footman said he thought he'd seen her leave the house." He shook his head as though to banish dark thoughts. "I'm just glad she's all right."

"'Course she is, my lord. The young lady caught her right quick. The wee bairn was safe in her care," Mrs. Finch told Lord Forres.

"Why don't I take the lass inside for a bite to eat and a

nap?" Mrs. Finch reached for Blair, but Forres didn't immediately hand his daughter over. When he finally did, it was with a sigh and great reluctance.

"Be a good girl, Blair." He chucked her under the chin and the little girl bobbled up and down in her nurse's arms.

Rowena watched this familial intimacy, her heart flipping inside her chest. Mrs. Finch started to walk back toward the main house, and as she passed by Rowena, Blair reached out with one chubby little hand and waved at her before resting her cheek on Mrs. Finch's shoulder. A strange pull in her made her want to rush after the child.

The Earl of Forres cleared his throat and Rowena came back to herself.

"Have you been enjoying the house party, Lord Forres?" she asked, hoping that was the right course of conversation. It was the first time she'd been alone with a man besides her father or servants.

Alone with a man...

Rowena's heart tripped and she had to collect herself before she panicked. Her sister Milly had just gotten engaged early this morning, against her will, because a fortune hunter had snuck into her room the previous night and been caught by their mother. Nothing beyond that had happened, but it had been enough to scandalize them into marriage. Was being alone with Forres like this enough for a scandal?

"The party has been a pleasant distraction," Forres admitted.

She nodded. "Yes." She swallowed. Why was she so nervous? Normally she loved conversation and could talk about almost anything. Being alone with him left her tongue-tied and tingling as he drew near.

He held out the crook of his arm in silent invitation. The gesture was gentlemanly, but also natural and masculine.

The heat of a blush worked its way to her cheeks and Rowena didn't know what to do.

"Oh, come now, Miss Rowena, 'tis only my arm. I won't bite." He grinned at her and chomped his white teeth together in a mocking way.

A giggle escaped her, startling them both. Then he laughed, too, but there was a surprise in his expression as though he was astounded at his own amusement. The sound of his laugh was rich and warm and oddly comforting, given that he was a complete stranger. After only a brief hesitation, she placed her arm in his. Little tingles shot up her skin at the point of their connection.

"Allow me to escort you back to the house." Forres nodded toward the massive tan stone edifice of Hampton House. It reminded her so much of Pepperwirth Vale, her family estate only four miles away. Two ancient families, the Grahams and the Pepperwirths, had been neighbors for nearly two hundred years.

She and Forres walked in silence for a few steps before Forres spoke.

"I wish to thank you again for rescuing my daughter. Blair is..." He paused, and Rowena peeked up at him, noticing a slight ruddiness to his cheeks. "Blair is very precious to me. I'm afraid I'm overly protective of her."

"I understand, my lord. I was informed you'd lost your wife a year ago, my condolences. It must be hard for any parent to raise a child alone."

Forres halted and turned to face her, his eyes slightly wide in surprise. "Yes...yes, it is hard." He recovered himself. "Blair is a wee bit wild, as I was when I was a bairn."

Rowena couldn't resist smiling. "You were once a wee child?" Her own childhood had been full of adventures, as much as a well-bred English young lady could have had in the country, but she imagined Forres had a much more colorful life.

"Oh, aye..." His Scottish accent thickened to a richer brogue as he spoke. "I was always off in the woods or on a horse. My nurse couldn't keep me in a clean set of trousers to save my life." His solemn gray eyes held a hint of warmth as he led her through the maze of gardens.

"And little Blair is like you." Rowena laughed in

delight. The idea of the darling child running among the Scottish heather, wild and free, was a wonderful thought.

Forres nodded. "Yes, but she could use a wee bit of taming."

"Taming?" Rowena asked, tempted to smile. "All children need to be able to run free sometimes. I was often getting into scrapes when I was younger."

Forres gazed at her. "Now, that I cannot imagine! A proper young lady like you?" His expression was serious but there was a hint of gentle mocking in his tone. He was teasing her and she couldn't help but grin at him, temporarily forgetting how nervous he made her.

"Oh yes, I was a bit of a tree climber and I was always bringing home tadpoles, baby birds, and all other manner of fauna. I once nursed a baby deer back to health after its mother was killed one spring." She'd always loved taking care of wounded creatures great or small, and her parents had been thankfully indulgent of her desire to play the healer.

He covered her hand with his where it rested on his arm. "I was much the same. Always bringing home creatures. I rescued a pine marten one winter, raising the kit in my bedchamber beneath my parents' noses. It was a fine beast, a smart creature. He lived for nine years as a devoted pet, much to my mother's dismay."

"It must have been wonderful to grow up in a castle in

Scotland as a child." Rowena sighed dreamily, picturing the earl as a boy scampering about the woods.

"It was, but southern England here is just as beautiful. You live on the neighboring estate, don't you?"

"Yes, Pepperwirth Vale. It is a lovely house and all my memories there are happy ones." She was beginning to see just how fortunate she had been to grow up so loved and cherished and free of tragedy.

Before they could speak further, they'd reached the doors to the veranda at the back of Hampton House, and Rowena's mother was rushing toward her. Her mother, usually one to be immaculately dressed, was now wearing a wrinkled gown, her hair a bit frazzled. She must have been up all night worrying about Milly's situation.

"Rowena! Dear, you must come at once, your sister..." Her mother halted at the sight of Lord Forres standing beside Rowena, their arms still linked.

"Lord Forres." Lady Pepperwirth recovered, her strained features smoothing into a beautiful mask of pleasantry.

"Good morning, Lady Pepperwirth." Forres bowed.

"Er...yes, good morning, my lord. I'm so sorry for disrupting your walk with my daughter." Her gaze darted between them.

Forres seemed to sense her unease, and ever the gentleman, he took control of the situation.

"Shall I go speak with the staff regarding luncheon?"

"Oh yes, thank you, Lord Forres," Lady Pepperwirth exclaimed in relief.

Forres turned his focus to Rowena and heat flooded her cheeks when he took the hand that had been resting upon his arm and pressed a lingering kiss on her bare skin. When he released her hand, Rowena clutched it to her chest as she watched the handsome Scotsman stride away into the house.

"Well, that's certainly encouraging, isn't it?" Her mother glanced back at where Forres had gone.

With a little exasperated sigh, Rowena stared at her mother.

"He is very polite, Mama, but I don't think—"

"Oh hush, every man with good sense would be interested in you, dear. From the moment you were born, I knew you would grow up to be a beauty, just like your sister, but thank heavens you've a sweeter temperament."

"Mama!" Rowena protested. "You know Milly is as sweet as me. She simply doesn't suffer fools." Rowena adored her older sister but sometimes Milly acted a bit prickly, especially to young men, because she feared marriage and the loss of her sense of self. It was a complicated notion, but Rowena understood that Milly feared a husband would repress her freedom.

Lady Pepperwirth puffed out her chest. "Yes, well, your sister has certainly gotten herself involved in a bit of trouble with her attitude. Your father and I have a fine mess to deal with getting a wedding arranged quickly with as little scandal as possible."

Guilt clawed at Rowena's insides and she pressed a hand to her stomach. Here she had been enjoying a walk with Lord Forres while her sister was no doubt suffering preparations for a wedding to a man she didn't know and didn't love.

It was my fault she was compromised. That part made Rowena feel even worse. The previous evening Milly had come to her and explained that she was worried that Owen Hadley, the handsome fortune hunter, had set his sights on Rowena. Unfortunately, Milly had been right about Owen and had been compromised when he'd snuck into her room by accident. It was their wedding her parents now had to plan.

"Does she really have to marry him?" The thought of her beloved sister trapped into a marriage because she'd been protecting Rowena...It made Rowena's stomach roll over.

"Of course she does," her mother said with a slight frown. "But don't worry about her, Rowena; she can use a bit of marriage to improve her mood. Mr. Hadley might be a suitable match after all. Now come, dear, tell me how you and Lord Forres met this morning."

Rowena rolled her eyes. Her mother was relentless when it came to marrying off her children. Unfortunately for her, Rowena wanted a love match.

"I don't think he is interested in me, Mama. He was being polite; that is all."

"Humph," her mother huffed. "Well, his land holdings in Forres are immense, his temperament is good, and he's a fine-looking man. We'd best snap him up before he takes his wife hunting to London."

Snap him up? That was the last thing she needed. A husband. Of course she wanted one, but she'd only just come out. A girl had every right to embrace the freedom of the city in the late fall, the dancing, the balls, the gowns, the suitors...Rowena did want to experience it at least once before she made a decision.

"Mama, I want to enjoy the Season. Must we discuss marriage *now*?" She knew she sounded a little childish, but she didn't want to rush such a monumental decision.

"Well, I suppose we have plenty of time to discuss Lord Forres later." Her mother's lips pursed. "I've come to tell you that your father and I must take Milly straight home to settle the wedding plans. You are to remain here at Hampton for the duration of the party. The dowager countess will be a diligent chaperone for you."

Her parents were leaving? Rowena clutched her mother's arm. "But you can't go, Mama. I need you here—"

"Nonsense. It's time you were off my leading strings and on your own for a bit. We won't be far." Lady Pepperwirth patted her hand gently.

Following her inside the grand Hampton House,

Rowena paused in the entry. The muted gold light coming in through the vast windows illuminated the grand staircase. Only last night she'd descended those steps as a debutante in a white gown, the eyes of every man at the party fixed on her. She didn't revel in the attention, but it was pleasant to be noticed for once.

But the night was over, today was a new day, and she wondered what she was supposed to do without her mother or her sister here to guide her. Dinner was easy enough, discussions, courses of the meal, she'd learned it all, but...what was she to do during the day on her own?

"Oh, Milly, I wish I were you," Rowena murmured. "You'd know exactly what to do."

Chapter Two

Quinn MacCauley, the seventh earl of Forres, stared out of the wide French windows facing the veranda of Hampton House. The midmorning tea had just been laid out and a light luncheon was being prepared. Yet Quinn could not focus on these details. His mind, as it was wont to do this last year, drifted.

The ring finger on his left hand was bare, and he felt naked without the silver band he'd worn until a month ago.

Sweet Maura...

Had it truly been a year since his wife had died giving birth to the baby boy that had perished with her? He didn't feel ready to move on—he doubted he ever would—but Blair, his darling, wee bairn, needed a mother. She was growing up so fast, and before he knew it she'd be presented at court and suitors would be knocking at his door. As a single father, he feared he'd closet Blair away in a tower and not let her live a full life. It would happen all too soon, and knowing that made him hurt deep inside with a heavy ache of loneliness.

It was all of this that had him traipsing through England on a wife hunt. Any Scottish lass would have been fine, but he feared they would remind him of Maura. So he and Mrs. Finch had taken Blair and left Forres to come to England to find a woman.

He didn't expect to fall in love again, not after how he'd loved Maura. She was his childhood sweetheart, his dearest friend, his lover. The woman he'd chased through the wild heather and rode out on the grounds with every morning. The gaping hole in his heart was still raw. Absently, he rubbed his bare ring finger again as he watched Leo Graham, the Earl of Hampton, and his fiancée, Ivy Leighton, walk into the dining room. Their heads were bent toward one another as they shared whispers and secret smiles. The ache in his chest grew.

Ivy and Leo paused when they noticed him standing beside the windows.

"Forres! How the devil are you?" Leo beamed and strode over to Quinn, Ivy at his side.

"Good, Hampton. And you?" They'd only had a brief moment at dinner the previous evening to exchange greetings.

"Good." Leo smiled. "I'm delighted Mother thought to invite you down to the house for a few weeks before you travel to London."

Quinn nodded. "Aye, 'twas good of her to think of me." Leo's mother, the dowager countess, was a distant cousin of his. The convoluted bloodlines of the English and the Scots left him well connected to many of London's titled elite, including the Grahams.

"Well, seems like it will be just us for lunch. Mother isn't feeling too well, and the Pepperwirths are going home early. Hadley's leaving too; apparently we're to congratulate him on a wedding he needs to plan." Leo's lips twitched and Quinn sensed there was more to this situation than was being revealed, but he knew better than to pry.

"Oh, but, Leo, don't forget, Rowena is staying." Ivy nudged Leo in the ribs, her eyes darting between him and Quinn suggestively.

Leo's eyes widened as if finally reading his fiancée's thoughts, and then he coughed. "Er...yes, Rowena. You've met Miss Rowena, haven't you, Forres?"

Quinn nodded, amused that the couple in front of him seemed to be planning some attempt at matchmaking. Despite his heartache, he was finding the general hunt for a wife to be humorous. It was either laugh at his situation or cry, and he was not going to cry. He had shed his tears and was now determined to do what he needed to do for Blair.

As a Scot, he was a fair outsider to the English aristocracy's eccentricities with regard to courtship and marriage. Last night during dinner he'd watched the women in the room eye him appraisingly, and rather than be offended, he was surprised at how much it entertained him. The language of soft smiles and suggestive questions they posed to him, as though assessing his prospects for themselves or their daughters, had been amusing. And he had been just as interested in them for the same reason, attempting to see if any might prove a good match. But none at dinner had truly attracted him in the end. None except Rowena.

He couldn't help but rub his bare finger again as he thought of Rowena rescuing Blair from falling into the fountain. She'd saved his child and he wasn't going to forget that any time soon.

"Why don't you fetch her for luncheon, Lord Forres," Ivy suggested to him.

"I'd be happy to." Quinn nodded at them both. They were an attractive couple, Leo with his fair features and Ivy with her dark hair and olive skin. Like the sun and moon.

"Pardon me." Quinn left the dining room and walked down the corridor until he reached the main hall, where he froze, arrested by the sight of a woman alone by the stairs.

Rowena Pepperwirth stood directly in the path of a wide beam of sunlight coming through the high windows. Her pale gold hair glinted and shimmered like silk in the light. Her elaborate coiffure, with its coiled lengths done up in an artfully messy style, was so unlike the way Maura had worn her reddish brown hair. Quinn shook his head, banishing the comparison. They were different women and he should not compare her to his wife. He did not want a woman to replace Maura; he wanted someone new, someone who was her own woman.

"Oh, Milly." The young woman sighed. "I wish you were here; you'd know exactly what to do." Her voice was soft, a little husky, more womanly than girlish. She was young, a new debutante, but Rowena was a lovely woman coming into her own.

A little smiled curved Quinn's mouth up. She was more than lovely; she was exquisite. Her body was small in stature but with healthy curves. Rowena, at only eighteen, was perhaps naïve of the world, but she had been good with Blair. Natural mothering instincts. She'd make any man a fine wife...Quinn suddenly tensed as that thought occurred to him. That was not something he could just ignore, being as he was on the hunt for exactly that.

Leaning his shoulder against the wall, he studied her more closely. The white lace day gown she wore was dotted with smudges of dirt near her knees…where she'd leaned over the stone fountain to catch his daughter. A pink blush heightened the color in her cheeks as she wrung her hands, still talking to herself under her breath.

A few wisps of her hair came loose from the coiffure and dangled down her neck. An unexpected heated interest flooded his body as he pictured himself standing directly behind her, hands on her hips as he bent to nibble and kiss that neck. She would smell sweet, like rosewater, and her laugh as he kissed her would be breathless and husky. She would turn and curl her arms around his neck…Quinn blinked, shocked that he'd been lost in such thoughts. He hadn't felt attraction to any woman since Maura.

A moment later guilt followed and he ducked his head, drew a steadying breath, and focused on Rowena again. His primary hunt for a wife so far had been to study women with regard to their ability to be good mothers, but seeing Rowena now…it reminded him that any wife he took would also be his lover, not merely a mother to his children. It was a truth he could not ignore. He had been celibate since Maura died, but if he married again, especially if he took a woman like Rowena to wife, he would need to—would want to—consummate the marriage. Again that sense of guilt crawled beneath his skin.

Maura is gone, he reminded himself. Many widowers

moved on to new wives, but Quinn was finding it hard to imagine loving any other woman ever again.

I don't have to love her, but I can have an affection for her, enjoy her in my bed, can't I?

He regained his control and cleared his throat. Rowena jumped and whirled to face him.

"Lord Forres!" she gasped. "You startled me!"

He tried to calm her with a wave of his hand. The panic in her cornflower-blue eyes was something he regretted causing. He left the doorway to come over to her.

"I'm sorry, Miss Rowena. I came to fetch you for luncheon if you're ready." He crooked his arm, and, as he had in the garden earlier, after a brief hesitation, she placed her hand through it. It was a simple touch, nothing at all romantic in it—it wasn't as though he were pinning her against the wall and kissing her—yet he felt a forbidden thrill each time his and Rowena's bodies came into contact, even as innocently as this.

A strange stirring filled his chest. It was a curious sensation, one he had not felt since...since Blair had been born. Only then did Quinn recognize what it was: a nervous excitement. How odd that this young woman he barely knew could make him feel as such. It had been months since he'd felt much of anything. Only Blair brought him any joy.

"Do we...er..." Rowena nibbled her plump bottom lip

as though embarrassed to speak. He tried not to focus on her lips or how he had the sudden urge to nip them.

"What I meant to say is, do we have plans this afternoon?" Rowena ducked her head as she added, "This is my first house party and with my parents gone, I'm a little..."

"Out of your depth?" Quinn smiled. "I know exactly how you feel. A Scotsman doesn't always feel he is on steady ground once he crosses the border into England." He kept his tone light, teasing, and it earned a laugh from Rowena. The sound was musical, full of joy and relief. This fair English rose was an open creature, emotions plain upon her delicate features, and her eyes, such blue eyes that made a man thirsty to gaze upon, hid nothing of what was in her mind and heart.

"Thank heavens for that, my lord. I must admit, I'm nervous I will make a ninny of myself whilst my parents are gone." Her gentle, concerned confession tugged at his heart. The organ, so hardened into stone over the last year, jolted with an unexpected pulse.

"Do not worry, Miss Rowena, we shall survive the party together. At least today it shall be just us with Hampton and his bride-to-be. Four is not too intimidating a size for an afternoon." He almost covered her hand with his but caught himself. *I must behave. I cannot do more than offer my arm to her.*

"That is a relief. Leo, er...that is to say, Lord Hampton

is such a dear. And so is Ivy." Then her face turned a bright scarlet. "I ought not to call them that. I keep forgetting. Mama would be furious if she caught me not using titles. I always forget when it comes to my friends." She laughed at herself.

And there it was. That glimpse of who this woman was inside. A woman with a heart so open to friendliness and joy that she often called her friends by their Christian names. This was not the sort of woman he would find in London among the balls, dinners, and other engagements. Rowena was a rare and extraordinary creature.

"If that is the case, I'd much prefer if you called me Quinn. I, too, am not inclined toward formality when I can help it." A silly grin stretched his lips; he couldn't stop it. There was something about Rowena that caught him off guard and he relaxed around her.

Her blue eyes twinkled like the noon sunlight upon a loch's surface, sparkling with a kaleidoscope of colors.

"Then I will be Rowena to you," she replied, the red blush still staining her cheeks. "Oh look! Luncheon!" She nodded at the elegant setting as they entered the dining room.

The long mahogany table in the center of the room was set for only four places near the far end. A matching end piece sat against one wall, laden with dishes of cold turkey, lamb, pigeon, cold pie and ptarmigan, puddings, cheeses, biscuits, jellies, and fruit ready to be served. The soft pale green walls were decorated with portraits of the Hampton ancestors, who peered down at them from layers of oil.

Ivy and Leo were already serving themselves on small plates. A footman stood in the corner of the room, ready to assist if necessary. Ivy smoothed her bright blue tea gown with one hand as she saw them come in, and she broke into a wide smile.

"Rowena, come sit by me." Ivy patted the chair beside her.

Quinn kept his hold on Rowena's arm and walked over to the chair beside Ivy; then he released her in order to pull the chair back. Once she was seated, he leaned over a little, catching the hint of rosewater perfume she wore. Just like he'd imagined...

"Allow me to bring you a plate," he murmured.

Rowena glanced up at him, her eyes wide and delighted. "Thank you, Quinn." His name came off her lips so naturally, and his body warmed at simply hearing it.

Joining Leo at the side table, he fixed two plates, one for himself and one for Rowena, before he and Leo took their seats at the table.

"Now," Leo began with an amused glint in his eyes, "Ivy has just reminded me there is a wonderful old set of ruins we could ride up to and have a look around."

Quinn blinked. "Are you sure? It looks like rain." When he'd rushed out to the gardens earlier, he'd scented it upon the air. That crisp, clear aroma was unmistakably rain. White clouds hung low upon the distant horizon, but they weren't dark yet. Still, he knew when a storm was coming. It was a skill he'd attributed to living a life out of doors upon his estate at Forres. If there was one thing he knew about the English, it was that they played at being outdoorsmen, but most were too used to their pampered life of aristocratic splendor.

Scotland was harsh at times, the winters colder, the land less inclined to yield food. It made men stronger, and the women too. He glanced at Rowena again. Perhaps he was wrong to seek an English bride, one who was not used to such harsh environments. But the thought of hearing his name uttered in a familiar Scottish tongue and not have it be from Maura's lips...he could not bear it. No, better he marry an English lass because she would not remind him of what he'd lost. Again he stilled as he realized he was considering Rowena among his bridal prospects. But why shouldn't he? She was young, beautiful, sweet with Blair, intelligent...

"We'll take the Stanley. If it starts to rain, we can drive back. What do you say, Forres?"

With a shrug, Quinn settled in to eat his luncheon. "If the ladies wish to go, I'm happy to oblige."

"It does sound fun." Rowena grinned happily across the table at him. Her smile was infectious.

When he reached for the buttered toast, he noticed Ivy

was watching him, an intense but not unfriendly focus gleaming in her warm, dark eyes. He offered her a small smile, which she returned before focusing on Leo.

After the luncheon was over, the four of them retired to their chambers in order to dress more warmly for their outing. Quinn paused before the mirror close to his bed as he slid on his Chesterfield, a single-breasted coat of herringbone tweed. The velvet collar of the coat would keep his neck warm in case it did rain and a chill set in. His valet helped him tidy up his clothes before he exited his chambers. Hampton was just leaving his room and they descended the grand staircase together.

"Hampton, what do think of Miss Rowena?" Quinn slid his black leather gloves on as they reached the bottom stair.

Leo dug around in his coat until he found his own gloves. With a covert glance about the main hall, Leo leaned close to him.

"She's a lovely young woman, only just come out. Her presentation caused quite a stir in London. I imagine she won't be on the market long." Leo shot him a sideways glance as he propped one arm against the banister railing. "Mother thought you might be wife hunting. Is that true, Forres?"

Rather than be angered by the blunt question, he was amused at the thought of his intentions being uncovered by Leo's mother. She was undoubtedly shrewd.

"Truth be told, I am. Blair needs a mother and the running of my household has become a burden I would be glad to share with a wife." Since Maura had died, his sister had assumed the role, but Quinn was not blind. He'd seen Kenna mooning over wedding dresses in her fashion magazines from Paris and getting lost in daydreams of her own life. She deserved to have a chance to live and not suffer under any obligations Maura's death may have left her with. Therefore, Quinn *needed* a wife.

"Well, then," Leo chuckled, "Rowena would suit you very well. She's been trained to care for a large household, and I daresay she is affable too. But..." Leo paused, his eyes narrowing in speculation.

"But?" Quinn pressed.

Leo looked heavenward and sighed. "She's a romantic and a dreamer, Forres. If I have learned anything from Ivy, it's that you must let a woman be who she is meant to be. No clipping their wings, no binding them in marital shackles that would crush their spirits. The women of today are not like our mothers. They believe in equality and marriage as partnerships. Rowena is young but she'll be like her sister, opinionated and intelligent."

Quinn considered this and did not find fault with the idea. "A woman who knows her own mind is not a bad thing."

"Agreed," Leo said. "Rowena's natural sweetness hides

much, but do not be fooled. She will wish to run her own life as much as you do yours."

Quinn stared at Leo. Never had an Englishman been so frank with him before.

"Your observations are noted, Hampton. I'll be wise to remember your advice." He lowered his voice as he glimpsed a flutter of skirts at the top of the stairs.

Ivy appeared first, her lavender day gown with black trim a complement to her dark hair and olive-skinned complexion. She was hastily buttoning up a woolen overcoat. Quinn's eyes moved from her and all thoughts of Ivy and her loveliness were eclipsed when he caught a glimpse of Rowena.

He swallowed hard, strangely unable to speak as she descended the stairs. She wore a golden yellow gown, almost a rich mustard color, embroidered with red leaves on the hem and sleeves. Rather than wear a coat, she carried a gray plaid cape. Like a ray of sunlight, she seemed to float down the stairs in a brilliant splash of color. It took a moment for him to catch his breath.

"Do I look all right, Quinn?" She was staring down at herself in concern.

"Beg pardon?" Quinn finally got out as Rowena paused two steps above him. It placed her directly at eye level with him. He couldn't help but gaze at her rosy lips.

"You're staring, old boy," Leo muttered in his ear.

With a little jerk, Quinn uttered an apology. Rowena dropped his chin, her cheeks red.

"Let me." He reached for her cloak and she turned her back, letting him drape it around her shoulders.

"The Stanley is ready," Leo announced.

The group proceeded to the main door, which the butler opened. Leo escorted Ivy to the car.

"Quinn, do you mind sitting in the back with Miss Rowena?" he asked.

Sit next to a lovely woman? If he ever woke up one morning and answered no to that question, there was definitely something wrong with him.

"I'd be happy to," Quinn answered as he took charge of Rowena and lifted her up into the car's backseat. He was presented with a glimpse of her bottom, all too tempting, even covered by the bright yellow gown. A flare of unexpected arousal hit him like a bolt of lightning.

Must bury it deep. Quinn clenched his jaw and climbed into the car behind Rowena. He could survive one bloody afternoon, couldn't he?

Chapter Three

Afternoon sunlight bathed the crumbling ruins of the old castle with an almost ethereal glow. The distant clouds slowly building on the horizon forced the light to break through in shafts. The effect was lovely, the way the light pooled thickly in places and only glimmered in fading beams in others. Ivy leaves covered the gray stones, rippling at the barest caress of a breeze.

Rowena sighed, lost in dreams of what this old craggy edifice must have seen over the centuries. Knights astride white chargers, rushing along the sloping hill to the castle, fair maidens leaning out of windows, waiting for their men to come safely home.

"Beautiful, isn't it?" Quinn's husky brogue filled her ears. She spun around. He was standing right behind her, eyes drifting from one spot of the ruins to another before his gaze came to rest on her face. He smiled, a slight dimple in one cheek as he joined her beside what appeared to have once been a window. His smile hit her behind her knees as a fluttering sensation blossomed in her stomach. Rowena reached out to touch the stone window ledge behind her in an effort to steady herself.

Quinn's strong hands grasped her waist and lifted her up, setting her on the ledge so she faced him. She gripped his shoulders as her bottom touched the stone. The gray of his eyes was bright, like a mirror reflecting a beam of morning light. With the clouds in the distance, it seemed to make the world around the two of them full of sunshine.

"Quinn." She breathed his name, even more aware of how close they were. Her belly tightened with an excited tension she'd never felt before as he touched her. The way his hands, such large, capable hands, curled around her waist. He wasn't supposed to be doing this...putting his palms on her body, but, Lord, it left her dizzy-headed, and a tense excitement sparked deep inside her belly. It was scandalous, yet she wanted more.

He'd placed her eye level with him and she had all the time in the world to study him. The strong, stubborn cut of his jaw, the proud chin and straight nose. There was nothing weak about a man like Quinn. He was taller than Leo by a few inches and wider too. Such wide shoulders, her fingers curled into the layers of his coat. He wore no hat and the light breeze teased his dark hair into his eyes. He didn't move; his gaze was riveted on her face, a look of hunger there, a look she felt her own body mirrored. Her legs were parted slightly, her skirts tugged wide as he moved to stand between her knees, crowding her. Rather than be frightened, her breath caught in her throat and a slow, burning fire started in her abdomen, flushing her skin with heat.

He tilted his head, his eyes dropping to her lips, and she prayed he would kiss her. It was wild and inappropriate, but all she could think of in that moment was that she *wanted* him to do it.

Rowena licked her lips, suddenly remembering she ought to be behaving in the proper way, but none of Milly's lessons had prepared her for a situation like this. And she'd never been warned how she'd feel. It wasn't just that he was a handsome man. She'd met plenty in London. No, there was something about the haunted, intense look in his eyes as he gazed at her. Milly had often called her a hopeless romantic, and it was true. Rowena looked at Quinn and she felt the strong desire to heal him, to erase the pain that shadowed his face when he thought no one was looking.

But I am looking...and I want to help him.

"Forres!" Leo's distant shout shook Rowena out of her inner panic. "Where are you? We've set up a blanket with some lemonade and strawberries!"

"Oh goodness!" She pulled her hands off Quinn's shoulders and with a little shove, she hopped onto the ground, wincing when one of her ankles twinged on landing.

Quinn did not immediately step out of the way. Instead, she had to tilt her head back to gaze up at him, waiting for him to move. Never in her life had she felt so small, but Quinn made her feel...small. It was not bad. It was odd. It was as though he could easily lift her up and carry her off. The notion was silly, but it also sent little quivers of a forbidden thrill through her. She wished they hadn't been interrupted, but it was for the best; she'd been on the verge of doing something very foolish and very dangerous, like begging him to kiss her.

"Let me escort you," he murmured, his low voice a little gruff as he met her gaze.

They walked over the rocky path to where Leo and Ivy had set out a light picnic.

"There you are!" Ivy smiled. "I was worried you'd vanished. They say the fairies still roam these hills, you know." Her honey-brown eyes twinkled as she offered Rowena and Quinn plates of food.

Rowena settled herself onto the corner of the large woolen blanket, just a foot from Quinn. The small space between them seemed to crackle with energy and her body still hummed from that almost-kiss.

"Do you believe in fairies, Ivy?" Leo asked. He and

Quinn shared amused looks, one Rowena had seen upon her father's face too often. Indulgence and amusement.

Ivy continued to smile. "I suppose I do. Gypsy culture is full of superstition and beliefs. Fairies are a natural part of that."

Rowena nibbled on a bit of cheese as she studied the hilltop. It was easy to imagine a dozen glowing sprites dancing about the ruins, calling upon their magic to whisk away unsuspecting travelers. She caught Quinn's lips curled in a crooked, charming grin, as though he was inwardly laughing at the conversation. But the moment he noticed her watching him, the smile vanished and his eyes darkened with shadows again. Was he afraid to enjoy himself?

"What about you, Quinn?" she asked, curious to see what a Scottish lord would say.

"Oh, aye, the wee folk. I'd be lying if I said I dinna believe in them. There is a reason I never leave my daughter unattended for long. A human bairn is a prized trophy for the fairies." Quinn's tone was serious, but the glint in his eyes warned Rowena he was teasing her.

"Very funny," she laughed. The Scot chuckled and stole a glance at her, their eyes meeting. A flush crept across her skin and she prayed it would not pinken her cheeks too much. She'd known men could be snobbish, stubborn, and prideful—at least that had been her older sister's experience—but Quinn's behavior didn't fit with what her sister had said about men.

"Quinn, I believe we might be in the presence of two fairy queens ourselves." Leo chuckled and Ivy shot him a smile and everyone laughed.

The next half hour was pleasant and not too awkward as the four finished their picnic and talked about mutual friends back in London.

"I'll take the picnic basket back to the Stanley," Leo announced.

"I'll help you." Ivy collected the plates.

Quinn rose and stretched in a show of leonine grace. "I'd like one more tour about the ruins," he said.

Rowena watched Ivy and Leo preparing the basket, and they didn't seem to need her assistance. Could she be bold enough to offer to go with Quinn alone to see the ruins once more? She wanted to be with him again, just to talk, or not talk. It was so easy to be around him, yet he filled her with a wild excitement that she wanted to experience again.

Yes, yes, I can be bold. She squared her shoulders and stood.

"May I accompany you, Quinn?" Rowena asked, hating how breathless she sounded.

"Of course." He waved for her to join him. The thought of it sent a flurry of nervous butterflies through

Rowena. Was it being close to any man or *this* man that made her feel so...strangely excited?

They walked up the sloping hills and paused beside an archway. Below them the distant figures of Leo and Ivy were fast becoming as small as ants as they traipsed down the hills to the motorcar. The once-faraway clouds began to roll overhead. It would likely rain soon.

"Are you bound for London after this house party?" Rowena lifted her yellow skirts, following Quinn as he strolled idly through the crumbling edifice. She paused again by the window ledge he'd lifted her up onto earlier, remembering how having him hold her close had been...wonderful.

"I suppose," Quinn mused as he came around the other side of the window and leaned one elbow on the ledge to watch her.

"You are not certain, then?" A breeze tugged a lock of her pale hair free of its carefully arranged coiffure. Before she could tuck it safely back into place, Quinn reached over and stroked the unruly lock of hair behind her left ear. His warm fingertips lingered against the line of her jaw, the touch burning in a delicious way that made her tingle all over.

"I might stay here a while longer." Quinn's sensual lips parted slightly as his eyes dropped to her mouth. "If something persuades me to stay."

Without conscious thought, Rowena started to lean

forward, hoping he'd lean closer, too, and he'd kiss her. Her heart pounded as he stared at her lips and started to lean in—and that was when the skies overhead opened up and rain fell in the thick, hard sheets.

Damnation! She'd wanted to kiss him.

"Come, we must return to the car," Quinn ordered gruffly, briefly disappearing from view. Gasping, Rowena looked about for her plaid cloak. It was a particular favorite and she didn't want to lose it. The cold rain was thick and hard upon her skin as it poured from the clouds, forming a heavy mist upon the warm earth of the ruins.

"Devil take it," Rowena cursed, brushing her hair away from her face. The rain had tugged down the delicate coiffure and it hung lank about her shoulders. "Where did I leave that cloak?" She clutched her skirts, trying in vain to find the garment.

"Rowena?" Quinn's shout was muffled by the rumbling build of thunder. She'd have to leave it behind.

Lightning flashed above her, the bright light sharp and piercing. Her foot caught on a stone and she cried out as she fell. Something sharp twisted in her already hurting ankle and pain lanced up her entire leg.

Crack! The harsh clap of thunder was incredibly loud...

Scrambling into the shelter of the old crumbling stairwell in the castle, Rowena waited, soaked to the bone and shaking.

A figure emerged out of the heavy gloom. She sucked in a breath.

"There you are, lass!" Quinn barked in a harsh tone. "Come on, we've got to run to the car!" He joined her beneath the stairwell, sheltering himself from the storm.

"We can't go down; the lightning is too close. We're within striking distance. It's too dangerous." She gripped Quinn's right arm and jerked him down deeper into the safety of the stones.

Boom! Thunder, like cannons, temporarily deafened her ears. When the echoing rumble faded, she realized she was still clutching Quinn's arm.

"Very well, we ride out of the storm *together*." He settled in beside her and wrapped an arm around her shoulders. The instant warmth of his body lessened the shivers that had been building since it had started to rain.

Rowena buried her face in his chest, relishing the almost magical way he could make her feel warm and safe. A woman could get used to feeling like this with a man. She knew she was not like her sister; she was not strong or independent. She wished now more than anything that she had Milly's strength.

"I'm sorry, Quinn." She mumbled the words against his coat but he still heard her.

"Hush, lass. No one can tell how fast a storm will rise. We've all been caught unaware a time or two. At least you had the sense to take shelter here." As he spoke, his arm tightened about her body and she crawled even closer to him.

Rain fell hard all around them but the craggy stones were strong against the flowing rivers that made thick puddles amid the ruins. The thought of all that cold water made her tremble harder.

"You're shaking hard enough to rattle even my bones, lass. Come here." Quinn chuckled, and without warning, he scooped her up and settled her over his lap. She wrapped her arms around his neck, sighing at the delicious heat of his body despite the chill of their wet clothes.

"Perhaps we could distract each other," she suggested as her teeth began to chatter from the chill. "Would you tell me about Forres? I've never been to Scotland." Rowena raised her head, meeting his gaze. Those gray eyes of his were like the thundering clouds above, churning, tempestuous, but it was all trapped inside him. Did he miss home? Did he miss his wife? Rowena couldn't fathom how hard such a loss must be. And now he was seeking a new woman, one who could ease his heartache, one who could raise his daughter with love. Rowena stared at his lips again, noticing how full and soft they looked. Everything else about the man was hard. But those lips promised soft, sweet, sensual things. A woman would do almost anything for that mouth to kiss hers.

"Forres is lovely in the summer," he replied, his tone husky, low, like a murmur of a lover in bed. "Heather covers the hills, and deep in the glens you catch a glimpse of red deer bucks wrestling for mates." Quinn lowered his head until an inch separated their mouths. Every part of Rowena's body tingled and sparked to life.

Please let him kiss me.

"Winter is beautiful." He was whispering now. "All the hot fires in the hearths." His brogue thickened and Rowena curled her fingers more tightly around his neck.

"Hot?" she echoed breathlessly.

"Burning...*scorching*..." That lightning heat was in his eyes as his lids lowered and his mouth covered hers.

Rowena shut her own eyes as his kiss exploded through her entire body. Her abdomen clenched and a queer throbbing started between her thighs as he parted her lips with a gentle, questing tongue. Rowena shyly responded by touching her own tongue to his. Was this how a kiss should be? So intimate? So sinful?

I don't care...it's wonderful. She melted into him, her fingers threading through his dark brown hair, tugging on the thick, silky strands as she sought to get closer.

A soft growl came from his throat as his kiss roughened and he angled her body back, allowing him to lean over her. The dominating hold he had over her sent fiery ripples through her. His mouth moved from her lips along her jaw down to her throat. Warm breath heated her skin and she moaned in helpless excitement.

"God's teeth, woman," he whispered in her ear before he bit the lobe.

Rowena jolted at the burst of pleasure deep inside her from the little love bite.

"Don't stop," she begged him as he feathered kisses over her cheeks, her eyelashes, then her mouth. It was strange, but she had the sense he was saying goodbye and that made her cling to him more fiercely.

"The rain is stopping, lass. We have to go for the car." He pressed one more kiss to her lips and then he set her back onto the ground beside him.

Shaking, but not from the chill in the air, Rowena watched Quinn get to his feet and peer out from the rocky stairwell to examine the skies. He was right. The storm was already passing.

And the brief heated passion they'd shared was fading as quickly as the mists around them.

With an outstretched hand, Quinn waited for her to stand. As they walked away from the ruins, she spotted her favorite cloak, which was now muddy and soaked. She ran over to it and picked it up, shaking some of the water out. Her ankle still stung a bit, but she ignored it. It was nothing compared to the emptiness in her chest when she glanced back at Quinn. There was a cool distance in his eyes that confused her. After what they'd just shared, she thought he would surely be warmer to her, or at least act more like a man interested in a woman.

Perhaps he isn't interested in me...but then why kiss me? As a distraction from the storm and nothing more? The emptiness in her transformed into a burning ache.

In the distance, the motorcar was humming and Ivy waved to them. "Hurry! We should get back to the house and warm up."

Quinn reached the Stanley first, opening the door for Rowena, and then he lifted her clear up into the backseat, drenched and muddy as she was.

"I'm terribly sorry, Leo. There's a bit of mud—"

"Nonsense." The earl waved a hand. "It'll clean up, I assure you."

"We were so worried." Ivy turned around in the seat of the car, her dark eyes wide as she studied them. "Good heavens. We need to get you both into hot baths at once, or you'll catch your death!"

Teeth chattering, Rowena could only nod. Without Quinn's body heat, she was frozen to the bone again. She peeped at him from beneath her lashes, feeling awfully silly. One kiss...they'd shared only one, and everything inside her felt alive, excited, and overjoyed. Yet his lips were pressed into a thin line and his features were brooding.

Am I a terrible kisser? Perhaps he had not enjoyed it the way she had. It was a sobering, unhappy thought that dragged her usual high spirits into great depths as they drove back to Hampton House.

I should not care about one kiss. It doesn't matter.

The lie was bittersweet, but she swallowed it down and raised her chin. It was the only way she would survive the remainder of the house party.

Who knew a kiss could prove so fatal to her happiness?

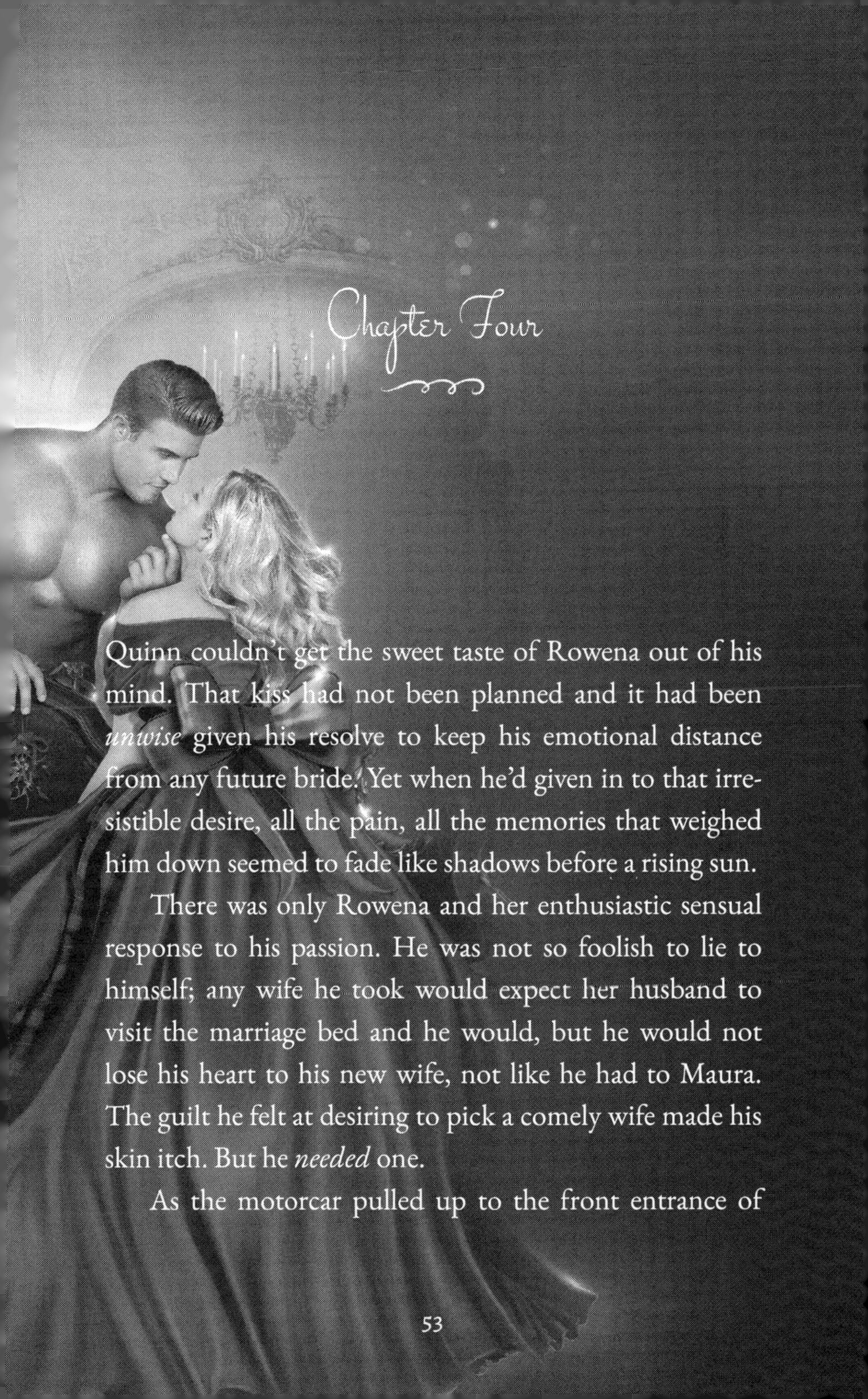

Chapter Four

Quinn couldn't get the sweet taste of Rowena out of his mind. That kiss had not been planned and it had been *unwise* given his resolve to keep his emotional distance from any future bride. Yet when he'd given in to that irresistible desire, all the pain, all the memories that weighed him down seemed to fade like shadows before a rising sun.

There was only Rowena and her enthusiastic sensual response to his passion. He was not so foolish to lie to himself; any wife he took would expect her husband to visit the marriage bed and he would, but he would not lose his heart to his new wife, not like he had to Maura. The guilt he felt at desiring to pick a comely wife made his skin itch. But he *needed* one.

As the motorcar pulled up to the front entrance of

Hampton House, he assisted Rowena from the vehicle and they walked in together.

"Papa!" A small, sweet, birdlike chirp caught his attention. Blair was rushing toward him as fast as her little legs could carry her.

"My wee heart." He opened his arms to her and caught her up as she reached him. Spinning with his child in his arms, he found Rowena studying him a few feet away, as adorable as a half-drowned kitten, shaking and needing to be held as much as his daughter did. Her blue eyes were wide and soft, a little smile curling her lips as she watched them. An emotion, one he recognized all too clearly, haunted her face. An aching loneliness.

Perhaps we are kindred spirits.

"Papa," Blair whispered against his neck in a way only a child could do. It melted away the ice in his heart. Hugging her close, he breathed in her scent.

"I beg your pardon, my lord. She's been anxious ever since the storm. Maybe now you're here she'll settle down for a nap." Blair's nurse trundled down the stairs, huffing and puffing. She was getting too old to keep up with a child. All the more reason to have a young wife.

"May I help with her?" Rowena asked. The hopeful look in her eyes was impossible to ignore.

"If you'd like." He shifted Blair in his arms and they walked up the stairs to his chambers. The nurse had seen to it that a wooden crib had been placed by his bed and that was where he tucked Blair in with extra blankets. He knew most people would have hidden their child away in a distant nursery while visiting a house, but he wanted Blair close. She was his world and he didn't want her out of reach.

"Papa is here; you can sleep now." He brushed her curls and she yawned, rubbing chubby fists against her eyes. Rowena stood beside him, peering down at Blair with open adoration.

"She is such a beautiful child."

"Thank you." He scrubbed a hand over his jaw as he finally made a decision. There was no need to go to London. Not if Rowena would consent to marry him. She was beautiful, sweet, and protective of his child, and she responded well to him physically. Yes, she would do well enough.

"Rowena, may I..." He gripped the cradle's edge and then sighed. "Could I speak with you on a delicate matter, alone?" When her brows drew together, he continued. "I'm aware of the impropriety but what I have to say is important."

"Of course, Quinn." She glanced at Blair, who had already fallen asleep nestled in her blankets.

"She's fine now. We can leave her."

Rowena left his chambers and he followed her to her own room.

"What would you like to speak to me about?" She

waited, poised and proper, except for her wet, bedraggled appearance. For some reason, he found he was fond of her looking imperfect. It was oddly charming. A wet lock of her hair hung like burnished gold against one cheek. He reached up and tucked it behind her ear.

"I'm not a romantic man. I'm sure I'm about to do this all wrong but I hope you'll at least give me a chance."

A faint wrinkle formed between her brows but she did not interrupt him.

"You know I am seeking a suitable bride. One who will love my child, and one who can take charge of my vast estate. I believe you would suit me very well."

Her lips parted and she blinked once. "I..." She swallowed. "Is this a proposal?" Her voice was soft, a little higher than usual.

"Er...yes." He shook his head and laughed. "I know we've really only spent a few hours together, but I trust what I feel and I see how you are with Blair." When she still said nothing and continued to stare at him in shock, he growled softly. "I've made a bloody mess of this. I should be on bended knee, professing my ardent love for you." That was something he could never do, but he couldn't bring himself to tell her that.

"Oh, you mustn't do that!" She covered her mouth, but not before he saw a shaky smile.

Quinn took one of her hands in his and lifted it to his lips. "Would you consider it? I do not need an answer right away, and I should speak to your father, of course, and—"

"Yes." The word was so soft he almost thought he'd imagined it. When he met her gaze, tears glinted, deepening the cornflower blue to a rich sapphire.

"Yes?"

She nodded slowly. "Yes. I will marry you."

He was relieved and...excited. "I'll speak to your father first thing tomorrow, then."

"Very well." She bit her lip, cheeks blushing to a rosy red. "Do we seal it with a kiss?"

Such hopefulness, such sweetness...he really couldn't say no.

"If you wish to."

"I do." She stepped closer and he needed no further urging.

Quinn closed the short space between them and curled one arm around her waist, tugging her against him. Her hands settled upon his chest as she tilted her head back. Uncaring of her now-ruined coiffure, he fisted one hand gently in the soft, damp coils of her hair and kissed her. He was no saint, could never profess to be, and she tasted too good to deny. And now that she'd agreed to be his, he couldn't help but feel possessive of her. This lovely lass, his lass, belonged to him. Slanting his mouth over hers, he deepened the kiss. Her sweet lips parted beneath his and their tongues touched, then dueled, and he wanted to take her there, damn the consequences. His arms banded tighter around her waist, his hunger for her growing. Her curves were soft as she pressed against him, and he had that animal urge to growl again. It did not escape his notice that it would be easy to scoop her up and lay her flat so he could—

Quinn jerked away from Rowena and muttered an apology.

"Is that normal?" She studied him, anxious lines forming on her youthful face.

"Is what?" He ran a hand through his hair, slicking back the wet strands to keep them out of his eyes.

"For a man to pull away. Am I not good at..." The words died upon her tongue and the way her cheeks blossomed with pink sent pangs of regret through him.

He'd been insensitive to her by pulling away. She had no knowledge of men or their proper behavior. She was but eighteen. He'd lived an entire decade longer, had been married, and had lived fully in the world. The wounded expression in her eyes cut him with a surprising sharpness.

"That is my fault. You're quite good at...er...that." And there were certainly a few things he could teach her, the wicked way tongues could play, how lips could tease or ravage...An entire world of kisses awaited her.

Clasping her hands together, Rowena glanced down at her little black boots. "Quite good..."

He sensed that still wasn't enough reassurance for his future bride.

"Rowena." Her name escaped his lips in a husky whisper. When she glanced up at him, he continued. "I'm attempting to be a gentleman. It isn't done for us to be alone; surely you know that. If I let my control go, it would overwhelm you. And we've only just agreed to an engagement. I am trying my damnedest to behave respectably." He almost laughed. If she only knew how kissing her frayed his control.

Her eyes brightened. "You feel it too?"

Feel it? He felt something dark and hungry whenever he got too close to her. Ghosts of long-dead passions he had vowed to banish after losing Maura stirred in the wings of closed-off corridors in his mind.

"I do. And until we are married, it makes me a dangerous man. I'm not so polite, nor so controlled as Hampton. You've been lucky to see me so well behaved these last few days. It's the Scot in me, I suppose." His chuckle was darker than he intended as he reached up to caress her cheek. It was a miracle she did not flee.

"Let me play the part of a gentleman for now. You deserve that, sweet Rowena." He gazed at her lips, a thirst for more of her sweeping through him.

"Promise me you won't cry off," she begged, catching his wrist.

"Why do you think I'd cry off?" He tilted his head.

"Because we've only just met and there's no reason you'd want to marry me..." The dejected look in her eyes stirred things within him he didn't want to face. But he did wish to reassure her.

"There'll be no crying off, especially not after kissing you like that, lass. I want you and I'm not going to change my mind." He brushed the pad of his thumb over her lips.

"I don't want this to be a dream when tomorrow comes." That damnable hope in her eyes made him feel wretched. She wanted to be loved, to be wooed, and he could only give her half of what she craved. Seduction, but no love. Yet he would claim Rowena as his, as selfish as it was.

"I would visit your father tonight, but I cannot miss out on the dowager countess's dinner. I promise, first thing on the morrow, I'll go to Pepperwirth Vale. What do you say to a wedding in one month?"

She beamed up at him. "I think that sounds wonderful."

He leaned down to press his lips to her forehead in a chaste kiss. His body shouted for a hundred other, not-so-innocent kisses, but tonight he would be the gentleman, even if it killed him.

"Good. It's settled, then. Now." He nodded at her. "Have your maid draw you a hot bath and warm up before dinner."

Quinn left Rowena's chamber, not looking back. He

knew his soul was black for taking advantage of her open heart, but she was the best choice for a wife and he could not let another man have her, not after he'd kissed her.

Rowena was *his*.

I'm going to marry Lord Forres. Quinn...

Rowena hugged herself and stared at the open doorway where he'd vanished moments before.

He does not love me; we are strangers after all. But I can win his love.

She believed this and ignored the dark little whispers at the corners of her mind. She relished the challenge of mending his broken heart. The romantic deep inside of her craved winning his love and knowing she'd helped him. Because, if she was being honest, he was an easy man to love, and she knew with certainty it was only a matter of time before she fell in love with him.

After a minute, she'd walked to the bathroom and rang for the maid to draw her a hot bath as Quinn had suggested. While she waited for the maid to arrive, she sat at the small desk in her room and wrote a hasty letter to Milly. She knew her sister would be concerned about her own wedding, but she hoped Milly would be happy that she, too, was to be married.

A young maid entered as Rowena blotted her letter and got up from the desk.

"Supper is at six, miss." The maid turned the taps on in the bath and tested the water with one hand while she talked. Rowena listened, but her mind was distant. Thoughts of the future already formed from the nebulous clouds of her daydreams. She was to be the Countess of Forres. And she was to be a mother to a darling child. She would be living with a man who needed her and a daughter who needed her. She couldn't stop smiling as she climbed into the bath and soaked her cold muscles.

Two hours later, she was feeling refreshed and warm as she donned one of her favorite gowns. She had to look perfect tonight because she didn't want Quinn to regret proposing to her. The train was embroidered with gilt-colored peacock feathers, and black beadwork accented the blue bodice. It was one of her post-court presentation gowns, which she'd worn only once before. The last time she'd walked into a room wearing this gown, every man had gazed at her with longing and every woman with envy. Tonight, she cared only about Quinn.

Rowena checked her bodice carefully, tugging at the slightly risqué neckline before she pulled on her sapphire-blue silk elbow-length gloves. The young maid behind her worked in concentrated silence on her hairstyle before adding a headpiece. A trio of feathers made of white gold and diamonds was tucked securely in the back of her coiffure like a Spanish comb.

"The gentleman will be speechless." The maid smiled.

"I look presentable, then?" she teased the maid. They were close in age and Rowena was never shy about making friends, no matter their social status.

"Oh yes, miss. Like as not, they'll forget all about dinner when they see you."

"Good." Rowena rose from the vanity table and tweaked her gloves before exiting the chamber.

This time she would face the main stairs alone. No Milly would be there to guide her. She was on her own.

I ought to get used to this if I am to be mistress of my own house in a few months.

A flutter of nerves stirred like restless bees in her stomach at the thought. She paused at the top stair and looked down. The party had shrunk to six: Leo; Ivy; Ivy's father, Mr. Leighton; and the dowager countess. And then there was Quinn, of course. All of the guests were gathered at the foot of the stairs. Quinn was deep in discussion with Mr. Leighton. He cut a dashing figure in his black evening dress suit. The white pique shirt and black trousers were perfectly pressed and he wore a white tie. It was the costume of a gentleman, but his dark hair was a tad long and ruffled, as though he'd gone riding upon the open moors before dressing for dinner.

Rowena took a moment to drink in the sight of him. This handsome Scottish lord was to be hers, just in time for Christmas. A silly smile curved her lips as she watched Quinn throw his head back in laughter at something Mr. Leighton said. The two men clapped each other's shoulders in a warm gesture before talk quieted. Quinn turned toward the stairs.

Her heart gave a little flip in her chest when their eyes met.

Hunger darkened his silver eyes as she descended the stairs and drew closer to him.

He will love me. I know he will. She would win her future husband's heart. It was a promise she would do anything to keep.

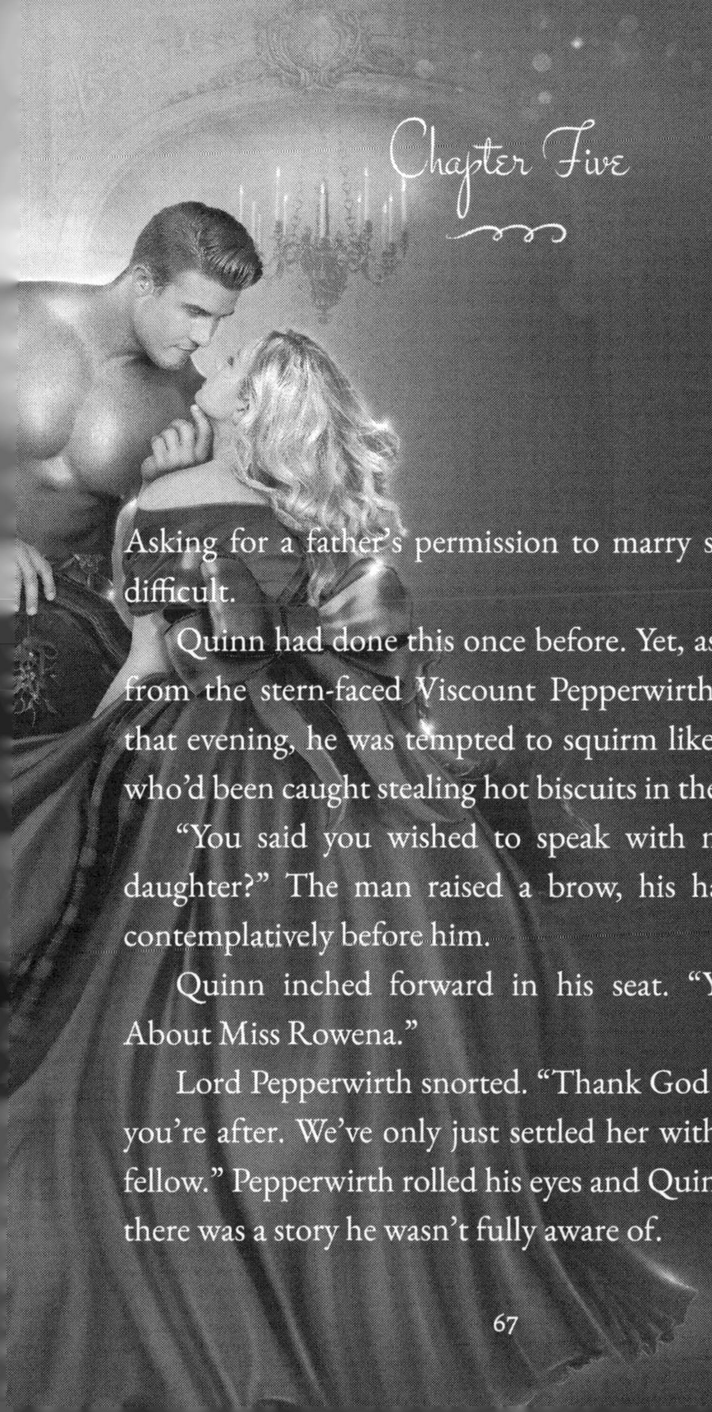

Chapter Five

Asking for a father's permission to marry should *not* be difficult.

Quinn had done this once before. Yet, as he sat across from the stern-faced Viscount Pepperwirth after dinner that evening, he was tempted to squirm like a young boy who'd been caught stealing hot biscuits in the kitchens.

"You said you wished to speak with me about my daughter?" The man raised a brow, his hands steepled contemplatively before him.

Quinn inched forward in his seat. "Yes, my lord. About Miss Rowena."

Lord Pepperwirth snorted. "Thank God it's not Milly you're after. We've only just settled her with that Hadley fellow." Pepperwirth rolled his eyes and Quinn sensed that there was a story he wasn't fully aware of.

"So, Rowena..." Pepperwirth waved a hand for him to continue.

Lord, Rowena's father wasn't making this easy.

"I've spoken to her this past evening. With your blessing, I should like to marry her in a month's time."

Lord Pepperwirth did not react for several long seconds. Instead he closed his eyes, then opened them again after a while. The grandfather clock in the corner of the study ticked away, marking the seconds of silence.

"Rowena has agreed?"

"Aye." Quinn nodded, his palms slightly sweaty. He rubbed them on his trousers. This was not going well.

"You have a title, Lord Forres, and a well-run estate, so I'm told. You also have a child from your first wife, correct?"

"Yes, but—"

Pepperwirth silenced him with a hand. "You've known my daughter all of three days before you proposed. Any father who loved his child would have to question a suitor's motives under such circumstances."

Balling his fists, Quinn growled softly as he leaned forward in his chair. "If you are questioning my honor and my intentions, my lord, then know that I have not and would not do anything to the lass that I should not."

Pepperwirth stood firm in the wake of Quinn's attitude, where weaker men had run scrambling for the hills.

"Then tell me, Lord Forres, do you love my daughter?

I do not agree to part with my youngest child unless I am assured she will be loved. You will understand once your own child is facing suitors and you sit where I do. Rowena's happiness is what matters to me."

"Then you must ask *her* why she agreed to marry me." Quinn was on his feet, scowling down at Rowena's father.

"Sit down, Forres. I'm not arguing with you. I'm merely trying to ascertain the situation." Pepperwirth leaned back in his chair, a knowing glint in his eyes that made Quinn's skin prickle as he sat back down.

"So you do not love my daughter. Why ask for her hand, then?"

This time it was Quinn who shut his eyes. How could he tell this man what was in his heart when he barely understood himself? He wanted Lord Pepperwirth to understand that he would treat Rowena with respect and affection, but he wasn't sure he could love again. Blowing out a slow breath, he faced Rowena's father and spoke the truth.

"She is not like other women. There is a compassion in her, a love for my child, a bairn she does not even know, and though she is young, she is intelligent. I find much that pleases me in her smile, the way she laughs, and how when she looks at me, I do not feel..." His throat constricted but he continued. "I do not feel so broken." It was true, this sudden realization. Rowena made him forget the past. She blocked it out, made him feel new and not burdened with things that had broken his spirit a year ago.

Lord Pepperwirth pushed his chair back and rose, holding out a hand to Quinn.

"Very well, you have my blessing. If this is truly what Rowena wishes, then I agree. We have plans to marry my eldest, Milly, to Hadley in three weeks. Would you and Rowena mind waiting until early December to be married? That would give me time to settle her dowry and for you to make your own preparations in Forres."

Quinn shook Pepperwirth's hand. "That would be suitable. I'll escort my daughter home and return in early December. I trust you will post the banns for us."

"Yes, of course," Pepperwirth said as he walked around the edge of his desk and escorted Quinn to the door. "You may tell Rowena you have my blessing. No doubt she'll wish to prepare a trousseau and see to the remaining wedding arrangements."

"Thank you." Quinn departed from the study and nearly stumbled into his fiancée.

"Quinn!" She grinned, her bright eyes twinkling. "How did it go? What did he say?" She looped her arm into his so casually that he thought for a moment she'd been doing it for years. Her pleated skirts swirled as she kept pace with him while they walked.

"It went well. We are to wait until early December for the wedding. I must go. I have to make all the necessary preparations. You can manage the rest here, can you not?"

Rowena's smile faded. "Oh, well, yes, I can. Will you be gone long?"

He was going to crush that endearing hope in her eyes, but it wasn't to be helped. He had business to see to in Scotland and preparations to make for his new bride. And he needed some time to adjust to this new development in his life. The past few days they'd become too...close for his liking. He needed to firm up his walls, defend himself, or else the blue-eyed sprite would crumble his resolve to keep his emotional distance.

"Unfortunately, I won't return until a day before the wedding. There is much to be done." He paused at the front door, where a butler already stood waiting with his coat and hat.

She was watching him with a hesitant and hopeful look that tore at his frozen heart.

"Quinn, could you not come a few days sooner?" Her voice was soft and a little husky with emotions she was valiantly trying to bury.

It would be so much easier for them both if she hadn't fallen in love with him...but she had. He could see it shining from the depths of her too-blue eyes.

"Perhaps," he answered. "But do not depend on it. I've been away from Forres too long and..." He let the butler help him into his coat and then he settled his hat upon his head. A motorcar was waiting to take him back to Hampton House, where he would retrieve Blair and Mrs. Finch and travel to the train station.

"Quinn." Rowena's whisper was a gentle plea he could not ignore. Without a care to the butler standing only a few feet away, Quinn cupped Rowena's face with one hand and captured her lips. He intended the kiss to be sweet and chaste...but as always, Rowena's taste exploded upon his tongue and robbed him of his good sense. The kiss turned hungry between them, nearly burning through him like an out-of-control fire. Damn, the woman was nigh impossible to resist.

Only after a delicate cough from the butler did he finally break away from Rowena. Her lips were a little swollen from his kiss and she was smiling again. That was what he wanted. Only smiles. Brushing his thumb over her lips, he whispered a murmured goodbye and fled, in the most gentlemanly fashion, to the waiting motorcar.

Time away is what I need. Time enough to remember that my own wants and needs must come second. This is to be a marriage of convenience, not of love.

Rowena fingered the fine lace of her wedding gown as she waited for her grand entrance into the chapel in the small parish of Hampton. Had it only been two months since she had agreed to marry Quinn? So much had happened between then and now. She'd watched her sister marry Mr. Hadley and leave for his estate in the Cotswolds. The only thing that had eased the ache of knowing she and Milly were facing separate lives was the fact that she had a new family now, one that would be hers forever.

"Rowena, love, are you truly ready for this?" Her father's blue eyes were dark with emotions he usually hid. A glint of tears was there, too, and seeing that made her own eyes burn.

"I'm ready, Papa. I love him. I did not know I could fall so fast, nor so hard, but I have." She blinked away tears. "He needs me. I have to save him." It was so hard to tell her father what lay in her heart. There was a wild jumble of emotions that made little sense to her. She only knew that loving Quinn was her destiny and that she had to heal that dark, bruised, and broken part of his soul he was determined to hide from her.

Her father smiled sadly. "Always my brave little child, aren't you?" He pressed a kiss to her temple and then held out his arm. "The music is playing. I believe it's time."

The doors opened in front of them and she was met with crowded rows of pews on both sides. Friends and family were peering back at her with smiles as she began to walk forward. A cold breeze from outside followed her along the middle aisle, stirring the red rose petals covering the aisle to the altar. They looked like red blood, and Rowena had the strangest sense that it was somehow an omen of her future.

I'm not afraid.

She raised her eyes from the fallen petals to the altar. Quinn stood at the front of the church. He wore a lovely red tartan kilt and a dress coat. It was the first time she'd really seen his legs, the muscled calves a sign of the strength he'd also hidden. He waited for her now, like a Celtic warrior of old, to claim her as his bride. Rowena's steps quickened but her father gently and firmly made her keep a reasonable pace when she would have sprinted straight to Quinn.

When she finally reached her fiancé, she offered him a smile. The priest stood between them, speaking the words of the ceremony. She had to focus on her breathing as they exchanged vows and Quinn placed a gold band on her finger. At that simple, yet so crucial touch, her skin tingled with a muted warmth, like long hours spent drowsy and half awake beneath a pile of woolen blankets when she slept in. It was a happy sensation, one that comforted her beyond measure. Quinn murmured his vows, his silver eyes sharp on her face as he focused entirely on her.

And then he was kissing her. She felt rooted to the ground, yet floating at the same time. It was a delicate kiss, as though she were brushing her lips against the downy feathers of one of her mother's fans. The memory filled her with a bittersweet ache as she kissed Quinn. He was her husband now, and she would make new memories in her new home.

"Are you all right?" Quinn's whisper ran over her skin like silk. He wrapped one strong arm around her waist and held her close.

"Yes, thank you." She sniffed and blinked, forcing a smile upon her lips. "I just realized I will miss my home."

The gray of Quinn's eyes softened, like the undercoat of a mourning dove. "You will make Forres your home now. Whatever you wish to do, I can arrange. I want you to be happy, Wife." He gave her waist a soft pat and he smiled that winning grin that assured her she would have a chance to make him happy too.

As the priest pronounced them married, they descended the steps and walked down the aisle arm in arm. There had been a wedding breakfast before the ceremony, a little unusual, but Quinn had wished to leave almost immediately. He'd returned to England with his own car just in time for the wedding, making the long journey alone. Together, they would drive all day to reach Edinburgh by night, where they would stay at an inn before completing the journey to Forres.

Rowena and Quinn climbed into the carriage, which took them from the church to Pepperwirth Vale; there they would change into their travel clothes. Milly and Owen were among the first to greet them upon returning from the church. At the sight of her, Rowena ran toward her, her throat tight.

"Milly!" she gasped, hugging her sister, uncaring of the delicate fabric of her wedding gown. All of a sudden, a sob tore through her throat and she buried her face in Milly's neck.

"There, there, Rowena, I'm here." Milly ushered her inside to a parlor where they could be alone to talk. The men did not follow them and Rowena sagged in relief. She didn't want Quinn to see her like this.

"Tears on your wedding day? Come now, Rowena, dear. What's the matter?" her sister teased, and held out a handkerchief.

"Oh, Milly. I shouldn't be so silly, but I can't seem to..." Rowena dabbed at her eyes with the cloth and sighed as she collapsed into the nearest armchair.

"Owen says Forres is a good fellow. Is that not the case?" Her sister knelt on the floor beside her, peering at her intensely.

"It isn't that. I am afraid to leave home. Did you feel that way?"

Milly laughed, a soft twinkle in her eyes. "I did. I remember looking back at the house as we drove away and thinking of how awful it was. But then we reached Owen's house and...it was love at first sight. The place was in need of many repairs, but I loved that I would be making it my home as I fixed it up. Don't be afraid to do that with your new home. Embrace it all with excitement."

Her sister was right. Of course she was. Rowena dried her eyes and handed the damp handkerchief back to Milly.

"Are you and Owen happy now? I know that you despised him and that you didn't want to marry him." She didn't want to resurrect her sister's pain, but she needed reassurance that things would get better.

A lovely, dreamy-eyed expression took over Milly's face. "He was the last man on earth I would have married, but now...I can't imagine life without him."

Rowena stared at Milly in shock. Her sister had always been vocal about her views on men and marriage. Yet here she was, smiling and almost giddy over a man. If marriage made Milly happy, maybe it would do the same for her and Quinn. She desperately hoped so. All she wanted was to win his heart.

Rowena rose from the chair and embraced her sister again. Ever since she was a child, hugging Milly had always been a comfort to her. The bond they shared was invisible but unbreakable.

"I wish you were coming with me to Scotland. I've never been on my own before."

Her sister pinched her cheek playfully. "That won't stop you, Rowena. You forget I know you. Anyone who meets you wants to be your friend. Once you reach Forres, you'll make friends. You'll build a life, and Owen and I shall visit you."

Rowena swallowed thickly. "Promise?"

Milly held out a pinkie finger. "Promise."

They linked their fingers, giving them a little shake the way they'd done countless times growing up.

"Owen's always wanted to visit Scotland. If you need me sooner, send word and we'll come straightaway."

With that reassurance, Rowena smiled and plucked at her gown. "I ought to change. We have a long drive ahead of us. Quinn has to make the drive himself."

Milly *tsked*. "A smart man knows to hire a cab. It's much more enjoyable to share a ride in the back and cuddle with one's husband."

"Cuddle? You?" Rowena couldn't contain the plague of giggles that followed.

Milly promptly pinched her waist in retaliation but she was smiling.

"Yes, and you ought to try that with Lord Forres. He doesn't look like a man who cuddles, but neither does Owen, and yet he's wondrously splendid at it." Pink stained Milly's cheeks but she continued to grin as she followed Rowena to the door.

Rowena rushed upstairs to change and have a footman bring her travel valise down. The remaining trunks containing her wardrobe would be brought to Forres in a few days. Rowena selected a navy blue pleated skirt and a white blouse. Sensible and perfect for a long day in the car. She laced her black boots and left her bedroom. She paused in the doorway to look back at the room where she'd spent most of her life. A young woman's bedroom.

No longer mine.

Now she was to have a new room, one she would share with her husband. She tried to let excitement fill her and bury the aching sadness at leaving her home behind.

I must look forward.

By the time she'd come back downstairs, she found Quinn had changed from his wedding suit to his own travel clothes. Her parents were waiting at the entrance along with her sister and Owen.

Rowena lifted her chin and met them all bravely. She would not cry, not on her first day as a married woman. Milly and Owen followed Quinn outside to the waiting car and left Rowena alone with her mother and father.

The Pepperwirths had always been a sensible family, but they loved deeply. Now she saw that love in the tears that coated her mother's cheeks.

"You will write to me the moment you arrive at Forres. I want to hear all about your rooms and the estate. Make sure you go to the village and hire a lady's maid immediately since your sister took Constance." Her mother was doing her best to sound businesslike but Rowena heard the catch in her voice.

"Of course, Mama." Rowena hugged her fiercely, shutting her eyes tight to stop any tears from falling. Her nose tingled as she tried to control her sadness.

When she faced her father, she choked back a little gasp. The heartbreak in his eyes was stark and shocking.

"Rowena." He murmured her name and held out his arms. She rushed into his embrace and he kissed her forehead. "My darling girl, whatever will I do without you?"

Rowena chuckled, but she had to swallow hard before she could speak.

"You'll miss me, as I will miss you, which is why you must come up to Forres for Christmas. You will, won't you?"

"If it's all right with Forres, then we will."

"I'm sure he'll be happy to have you."

Her father's gaze darkened with an unusual solemnity. "Rowena, I consented to this marriage because you love him, but..." He paused and Rowena felt her stomach twist into knots. "He's a man who's suffered a great and terrible loss in his life. A loss so deep it would break any man. I hope you will prepare yourself for what lies ahead."

Rowena nodded. Quinn's first wife, that's what he meant.

Her father continued. "Do not live in her shadow. Trying to be an echo of his lost wife is not the way to win his heart. Be true to yourself; he will love you as we do." Her father's bright blue eyes, the ones she'd inherited from him, shimmered with tears as he hugged her again and walked outside to join the others. Her mother held Rowena back when she would have followed.

"What your father didn't tell you was that a man's heart can sometimes be won by an open, honest, and happy lover." She gazed meaningfully at Rowena.

"What do you mean, Mama?" A flush crept along her skin. It was quite unexpected to have this sort of discussion with one's mother, but the information had to be worth the embarrassment.

"Do not be afraid of passion. Open yourself up to it. There will be so much you will learn about what transpires between a man and his wife, but the more you love each other, the greater the reward. Embrace it and him and you'll win his heart."

Rowena had already tasted a hint of Quinn's passion and had no intention of denying herself of it. Her mother walked with her outside, and with a few last hugs, she climbed into the motorcar beside Quinn and waved goodbye to the life that had once been hers.

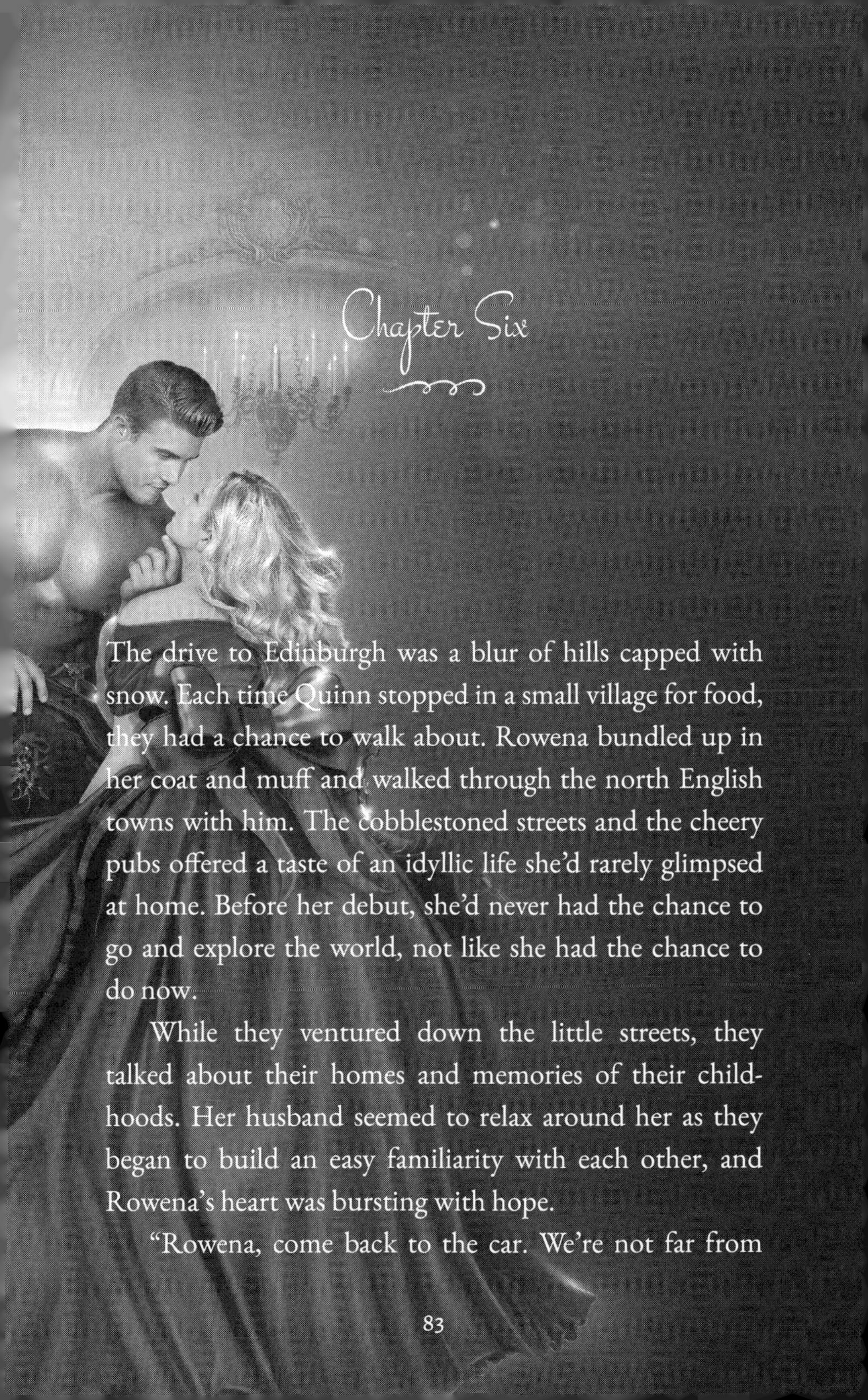

Chapter Six

The drive to Edinburgh was a blur of hills capped with snow. Each time Quinn stopped in a small village for food, they had a chance to walk about. Rowena bundled up in her coat and muff and walked through the north English towns with him. The cobblestoned streets and the cheery pubs offered a taste of an idyllic life she'd rarely glimpsed at home. Before her debut, she'd never had the chance to go and explore the world, not like she had the chance to do now.

While they ventured down the little streets, they talked about their homes and memories of their childhoods. Her husband seemed to relax around her as they began to build an easy familiarity with each other, and Rowena's heart was bursting with hope.

"Rowena, come back to the car. We're not far from

Edinburgh." Quinn stood by the vehicle, the door open, one foot braced on the car's interior. He looked incredibly dashing with the buttons of his long, thick coat undone to show the shirt he wore, and his dark hair tousled by the wintry air. It never ceased to amaze her that this man was all hers.

"Coming!" She rushed along the snowy walkway, skidding into him. He caught her in his arms and she laughed, brushing a kiss on his lips.

His eyes widened in surprise before he returned the kiss. Rowena melted into him, playing with his mouth as he'd taught her to do. The embrace and the kiss heated her, just as the warm fire in her bedroom at Pepperwirth Vale used to do on cold winter nights.

With a little sigh, he broke the kiss and patted the small of her back. "We need to get going before it's too dark on the roads." He brushed a lock of hair back from her face.

Quinn tucked Rowena into her seat and made his way to the driver's side. As he settled in next to her, she pushed herself closer to him, resting her head on his shoulder, a delighted smile on her lips. It was silly, she knew, to feel quite happy in that moment of being with him when he did not love her yet, but she felt his heart was in reach. Rubbing her cheek against his shoulder, she yawned and tried to focus on the road. The wind blew the light snow in swirling gusts across the roadway, the headlamps illuminating the lovely dance of snow.

"Quinn, would you tell me about your family?" She knew so little of him and his life, yet she'd married him without truly knowing him.

"Well," he chuckled. "My father passed nigh on six years ago. My mother shortly thereafter. She missed the old man, you see. Now 'tis only me and my sister, and wee Blair, of course."

"Sister?" Rowena sat up, clutching his arm as she moved closer. Having another woman in the house, one she might grow close to like Milly, was wonderful. The thought sent a surge of joy through her.

"Yes, Kenna. She's two years older than you. Quite a troublesome creature, and I mean that in the best way." A grin softened the once-hard lines of his mouth. "She's always laughing and chasing Blair about the house. You'll like her."

"She sounds lovely. Does she have a beau?" Rowena couldn't imagine a happy, beautiful Scottish woman being unclaimed by a man.

"I suppose she does. Heaven knows she won't tell me but"—Quinn paused and glanced at her long enough to wink—"I believe the doctor in our village frequently receives accidental run-ins with Kenna when she goes to town."

"A doctor?" Rowena grinned cheekily. "Perhaps I ought to nudge them in the right direction." Meeting the doctor intrigued Rowena for two reasons: to see if she could help him and Kenna become closer and to see if she might help him in the village. She'd loved tending to animals and if there was any way she could help, she wanted to be useful.

Quinn laughed heartily. "If you like to play matchmaker, I'm sure Kenna would relish the help."

"Oh, Quinn, I'm so happy you have a sister!" She almost confessed to him how empty she felt at leaving Milly behind in England. The Cotswolds and Pepperwirth Vale were so far away from Scotland.

"You and your sister are close?" he asked, glancing her way before focusing back on the road.

"Yes, Milly has always been there for me. I don't know how I shall get on without her, but I suppose I must." She would. She knew she would, but it didn't ease the ache of missing her sister.

"You have me, and Kenna. And your sister is welcome to visit any time. I hope you know that." His gentle tone, so confident and welcoming, warmed her even more.

"Thank you, Quinn. I can't tell you how much that means to me." She squeezed his arm and placed her head back on his shoulder. Even though she felt comfortable with him now, there was a nervous tension building inside her as she realized they were getting closer and closer to their wedding night and all the things that would follow...

Her heart skipped a beat. Would he continue to kiss her with fire and passion? Or would he be quick about it? The sudden worry struck her hard enough to leave her feeling a little sick to her stomach. She frowned and glanced toward the window.

"We aren't far now. The inn we're staying at is just down this road."

They drove in silence for another half hour before the distant lights of Edinburgh appeared out of the night's gloom. Quinn drove to a small stone inn at the edge of town and parked the motorcar outside the front door.

"Go on in and tell the innkeeper we are here. There will be a room for us. I'll see to the car and luggage and be right behind you."

Rowena exited the car and rushed to the door, desperate to escape the cold. The stout wooden door creaked as she slipped inside the inn. Four long tables filled the common room, and they were full of men, most of them eating supper. The laughter and talking died away as their gazes turned her way. Rowena, still just inside the door, clutched her coat tighter about her body, her heart racing. She wasn't used to being alone in a room with so many men.

"'Ere now, how kin I 'elp ye?" A plump woman with a thick brogue and frazzled gray hair tucked under a white lace cap walked toward her, weaving through the tables, her apron spotted with flour and grease.

"My husband, Quinn MacCauley, said he rented a room?"

The men nearest her chuckled, roughly shoving each other with elbows and speaking Scots Gaelic, a language she recognized by the sound but not the words.

"Ignore them." The woman smacked one of the men upside the head and then waved Rowena to follow her as she headed for a set of stairs. As she walked past the last table, someone pinched her bottom. Rowena grasped and stumbled. The renewed raucous sounds of laughter followed her up the stairs and she bit her lip, mortified and more frightened. The spot on her bottom actually stung...

The innkeeper paused at the first room at the top of the stairs.

"Here's your room. The meals are served downstairs unless you wish to eat up here." The woman hesitated before holding out the key. "I suggest you stay up here. The men downstairs can be"—she met Rowena's gaze seriously—"a wee bit rough. Yes, you'd best stay up here."

Rowena closed her fingers around the brass key and watched the older woman retreat down the stairs. Then she tried to unlock the door to her room, but her hands shook.

Quinn, where are you? She didn't much fancy being so separated from Quinn, her bottom still stung, and she was uncomfortably aware of the noise from below—and her slim chances of being overheard should she need aid. The sound of footsteps on the stairs filled her with relief. Her husband had finally come in from the cold.

"Quinn, our room's here." She spun around and then gasped. A large, broad-chested man from downstairs lunged for her, a hungry glint in his eyes. There was nowhere for her to go. He slammed her against the wall, her head hitting the wood. Stars dotted her vision for a brief instant as pain exploded through her skull.

"Lovely English lassie," the man growled in her ear as he struggled to pull her skirts up. "Just wot I need to warm me up on a cold night, eh?"

Rowena screamed and clawed at his face, but her fingers were still covered by her fine kid gloves. She sucked in air, panic swamping her senses until everything around her seem to fog with delirious terror. The scent of ale and sweat mixed with his fetid breath clouded her lungs. His hand covered her mouth. Without a moment's hesitation, she bit down on his meaty hand, drawing blood.

"You little bit—"

A distant roar cut through the ringing in her ears. She glanced up to see Quinn racing toward her and the man towering above her.

"Touch my wife again and I'll bloody kill you!" Those were the only words he spoke before he launched through the air, tackling the lout to the ground with a sickening crunch.

Rowena winced at the sounds of fists pummeling flesh

and the grunts of pain from the man beneath Quinn. If he didn't stop hitting that man...*he could kill him.*

"Quinn, stop!" she pleaded. "Please stop! Don't kill him!" She grabbed Quinn by the shoulder, jerking hard on him. The blows stopped, and her husband, panting hard, glanced up at her, a snarl twisting his lips. Then, without saying anything, he got up, dragged the man to the top of the stairs by his legs, and kicked him over the lip of the stairs. The thumping sound of him rolling down the steps was strangely satisfying, and Rowena didn't like that she took a small measure of comfort from the final thud when the beast of a man hit the floor at the bottom. Quinn's shoulders relaxed and he turned back around to face her. When he approached her, he held his hands up as though he were approaching a wild, wounded creature.

"It's all right, Rowena, do not be scared," he whispered, his voice hoarse.

"I'm not," she replied, but her voice quivered.

Her entire body started to shake and suddenly she needed him, needed to be in his arms. She reached for him and he helped her to her feet. She didn't care if he didn't want to hold her; she clung to him, shaking, breathing so hard her lungs burned. When his arms circled around her, she melted into him and let go. She didn't cry, but she knew tears were going to soak his coat if she couldn't rally herself in a minute.

"I'm so sorry. I should not have left you alone. 'Tis my

fault. Please forgive me." He was murmuring these tender apologies in her ear, his warm breath making her shiver, and yet it soothed her too.

"May we please go into the room now? I believe I need to sit down." She tugged on his arms in pleading.

"Of course." He picked up the key from the ground, where she must have dropped it during the struggle, and helped her inside. The little room was cozy, with a bed large enough for two, a fireplace, and a small table for two with wingback chairs. Quinn helped her to the nearest chair and tucked her in with one of the blankets from the end of the bed.

"Wait here. I'll lock the door behind me." He bent, feathered a kiss upon her brow, and left their room. The click of the lock reassured her and she touched her aching cheek. A dull headache began to pound against her temples.

I'm not going to cry. She bit her lip and curled her arms around her waist, hugging herself to stop from shivering.

This was not her idea of a wonderful wedding night.

Quinn pounded down the inn's stairs and found the innkeeper checking on the man he'd beaten.

"Is he alive?" he growled.

The old woman shrugged. "Seems to be. Got a thick skull this one. Wot happened?"

Quinn kicked the unconscious man's foot.

"He attacked my wife. He's lucky I'm not in a killing mood because it's my wedding night. I want you to send for the magistrate. I intend to file a report against him and have this man taken into custody for assault. I'll prepare a statement and bring it down for you later." He walked over to the bar and reached for the most expensive bottle of Scotch he could find and held it up. "I'm taking this upstairs. Have a lad bring up our luggage and meals."

"Of course. It will be on the house, my lord." The woman nodded before glaring at the fallen man by the stairs.

Quinn stepped over the man and went back up to his room. He rapped his knuckles against the stout wood.

"Rowena, 'tis me." He heard sounds on the other side and then the lock clicked and Rowena's sweet face was peering up at him, fear still in her eyes. The sight of it made his blood boil. He should have been watching out for her the way he did Blair.

She stepped back as he entered and closed the door. "They're bringing up our travel cases and supper." He set the Scotch bottle down and reached for a pair of glasses from a table by the fireplace. Her teeth sank into her bottom lip as she watched him, and that youthful uncertainty tugged at his heart. This was not how she'd hoped her first night as a married woman would go. *Poor lamb.*

Quinn offered her a glass of Scotch and she took it, eyes wide. "Drink up. The Scotch will warm you while we wait for supper."

"Thank you," she murmured around the lip of the glass before she drank. She coughed and he patted her back.

"Second sip goes down smoother, I promise." He smiled and she returned it, although hers was a little shy.

"I'm so sorry I've ruined our night." She ducked her head, but Quinn curled a finger under her chin and lifted it. They were standing close and her sweet scent teased him.

"It is my duty to look after you. I've failed tonight and for that I'm so very sorry." He leaned down, intending to kiss her forehead, but she reached up and caught the back of his neck with one hand, pulling his head down a few inches as she kissed him.

Petal-soft lips and a warm, exploring little tongue stroked at his mouth. He had *missed* this, the intimacy between a man and a woman. Rowena's sweet, sensual exploration lit his body on fire and old hungers he'd repressed for the last year surged back to the surface. Quinn's body tensed as he wrapped his arms around her and lifted her off the floor, intending to carry her back to the bed.

A quick knock on the door had them both stumbling apart. Rowena was smiling again, a little less shy. She covered her lips with her fingertips and wrapped her blanket around her body while he opened the door. A stout young man carried their two travel cases, and a little maid followed him, carrying a tray of soup, bread, and a bit of beef.

"Set them on the bed." He nodded at the lad and then took the tray from the maid and set it aside. He gave both servants a few coins and then locked the door behind them. When he turned back around, he saw Rowena was already nibbling delicately at the food.

"I hope you don't mind, I'm simply famished." Her cheeks pinkened as she realized he was watching her.

"No, please eat. I'll unpack us and then join you." He strode to the bed and opened his valise. He'd just lifted out his shirts when she spoke, her voice still tentative.

"Could we ring for someone to come light a fire?" she asked.

Quinn paused in the act of setting his clothes on the bed. A fire? Good God, he'd forgotten. He was so used to the cold that he rarely bothered with a fire until he was freezing, but his little English bride was from a southern part of the country.

"Of course. I'm sorry I didn't think of it." He abandoned the clothes and walked over to the fireplace and knelt down beside the stack of dry logs and the box with the tinder and matches.

"We really ought to stop apologizing to one another," Rowena laughed.

He chuckled as he arranged the logs and tinder and lit the fire. Once he was satisfied with the heating glow of the flames, he returned to unpacking. When he finally settled down in a chair beside Rowena, she was nestled in the blankets, her feet tucked up beneath her, the voluminous folds of her skirt flowing down over the chair to the floor.

"Did you get enough to eat?" he asked between bites of his brown soda bread.

"Hmm...," she replied in a sleepy murmur. Her head rested against the tall chair back as she gazed at him.

There was a gentleness to her, a sweet hopefulness for all the wonders life could give that made his heart hurt. He'd been like that once, a lad with only love in his heart. And then he'd lost Maura and the light that lit his world had been snuffed out. Blair had been his last bit of hope, until he'd met Rowena. When she'd agreed to marry him, an invisible burden that had weighed him down seemed to vanish. But he couldn't get close to her, not like he had Maura. There could be no more love; he could not survive losing another woman he loved.

Rowena stood up. "I'll change for bed," she murmured, and walked over to the bed to her travel case.

He had every intention of behaving like a gentleman,

but, well...he couldn't help it once he heard the rustle of cloth and the whisper of skin as his wife undressed. Flinging his head around, he snuck a glance. He started at the tempting sight of her corseted body and the flare of her hips as she dropped her skirt in a pool of dark cloth at her feet.

I would not be bad for assisting her...I have the right as husband, after all.

With a slow grin, he stood and faced Rowena.

Chapter Seven

"Allow me to help you." The soft words, deep and rich in that Scottish lilt, heated her blood.

Excitement flooded her and butterflies stormed through her stomach as she glanced at Quinn over her shoulder and shivered. She'd imagined this night a hundred times, how he might come to her, how it would go. She never dreamed he would offer to undress her. She'd always assumed she would have had a maid undress her and then she'd wait in her bed with nothing but a shift on. After that...well, she knew the basics of lovemaking thanks to her mother's explanations, but there was still so much she didn't know. When to kiss him...or was he the one to start the kissing...How was she to know what to do and when? Suddenly the flood of questions made her anxious and she twined her hands fretfully. Her heart beat harder and she licked her lips as she tried to calm herself.

Her body hungered for his in ways she still didn't fully understand, but she had to slow things today and find a way to enjoy tonight without rushing it. She wanted him to feel good that he'd chosen her as his bride, that she was a worldly and sensual woman, unafraid of their marriage bed.

"Would that be proper?" She was half teasing as she spun slowly to face him.

The wicked gleam mixed with primal hunger in his eyes erased all thoughts of any further teasing. Shyness crept in then, and her previous boldness seemed to fade. Perhaps she was supposed to do something, or say something...Did he really wish to undress her? What if he saw her body and did not like it? Shame heated her as that thought took hold. What if she wasn't beautiful or desirable in the way he'd hoped?

"Whatever you're thinking, lass, stop." His husky whisper sent riotous shivers through her. "This will be good between us, I promise you."

Good between us...She wanted that so much, not simply on a physical level but on an emotional one too. She wanted him to be happy with her, to enjoy being her husband both in bed and out.

For a moment they simply stared at one another before he stepped close to her, hands gripping her waist as he turned her around. Rowena trembled and held her breath as he plucked gently at the laces of her corset. The barest, briefest touches of heat where his fingertips brushed her skin burned like wild fire. When the corset was loose enough, she wriggled it down her body, desperate to be free of it quickly. She let it drop to her feet before nudging it with one foot out of the way. Her hands trembled as she fought not to cover her nakedness. Surely he would be pleased with her…He would still want her, wouldn't he?

"Lord, you're lovely." His voice was low and smooth like the Scotch they'd drunk earlier. Hearing him speak as he stood behind her was overwhelmingly erotic, her body humming. The flutter of nerves hadn't vanished, but she was excited to be with him, to experience everything she could with him.

"So are you," she replied, breathless.

His gaze raked over her body again and she saw the muscles of his shoulders tense as though he was struggling to stay in control. He removed their suitcases from the bed and set them on the floor. "Sit on the edge of the bed."

She turned to face him and stepped back until she bumped into the bed and sat down. The quilted blankets beneath her hands were soft and warm, soaking up the heat from the fire. When Quinn knelt in front of her, she resisted the urge to touch the dark hair of his bowed head.

He lifted her feet one at a time, unlacing the boots

before he slipped them off. She bit her lip, her heart racing as he cupped the heel of her bare foot and began to slide his hands up her leg to reach the hem of her stocking on her upper thigh.

He toyed with the lace garter with his fingertips, her breath catching before he slowly peeled the stocking from her leg, the fabric whispering off her skin, which was ablaze with the touch of his hand. As the first stocking fell from her toes, he landed a kiss on the top of her foot. Her entire body tingled with that single kiss. He smiled up at her before carefully repeating the process with her other foot.

"Scoot back a wee bit, love," he whispered huskily, and she scooted farther onto the middle of the bed.

"Very good," he praised. "Lie back." He was staring at her lap and she blushed, but stretched out.

She stared up at the ceiling, her heart racing, her body flushing with a wave of heat as his hands moved up her bare legs, pushing up the thin chemise. Cool air touched her between her thighs as he nudged her legs apart.

What was he going to—

Rowena gasped as he kissed her inner thigh. She panicked and tried to close her legs but he kept them open.

"Quinn, what—"

"Shh..." he whispered against her sensitive skin. "'Tis your first time. This will ease you, relax you for me."

Struggling to understand what he meant, she whimpered in pleasure and shock as his mouth touched her *there*. His tongue traced the sensitive folds and delved into her. Little pangs of pleasure so sharp they hurt spiked through her at every little lick of Quinn's tongue. The bedding wrinkled as she dug her nails into it, trying to find something to grasp so she didn't float away on the slowly building sense of bliss she knew was within reach.

Her chest heaved as she found it harder and harder to breathe, the sensual torture and the need for something almost at her fingertips...

His lips fastened onto the sensitive bud and she cried out as an explosion rippled through her. Her inner walls clamped down, but she still felt empty. She needed *more*; it wasn't enough.

Quinn rose to his feet and stripped out of his clothes. Rowena lay still, naked from the waist down, trying to recover her breath when she caught sight of her husband completely bare. The muscles she'd known were beneath his clothes were now exposed. He was no slender English aristocrat. He was all Scot, brawn and muscle with a hint of sunlight kissing his skin even in the winter. Her belly quivered in heady anticipation as she let her gaze drop below his waist. A thin, dark trail started a few inches below his navel and moved down to his groin.

He was large. *Too large*. He would not fit inside her...

"Easy, lass," he murmured as he came toward the bed.

Rowena scooted up to sit on the bed and swallowed.

"No need to be nervous," he teased as he reached for her chemise, the last bit of her clothes hiding her.

"Are all men as large as you?" she whispered, ducking her head to hide her flaming face.

"No," he chuckled. "And you honor me with such a compliment." He lifted the chemise off and tossed it to the floor. Then he pressed on her shoulders, urging her to lie on the bed again. She did so, but her entire body trembled. Quinn lay down beside her and propped his head on one hand as he gazed down at her.

"We have all night, and we won't do anything until you're ready," he said, and then bent his head, kissing her.

It was the sort of kiss that made a woman lose herself in dreams of warm fires and happy memories of being... loved. There was nothing selfish in his kiss. He gave himself over to the passion and to her. The barriers she knew he tried to keep in place were down for the moment. She reached up and cupped his jaw. A faint scrape of a nightbeard was forming and she nearly smiled. It would be like this every night. He would come to bed and she would kiss him, just like this. He would briefly open his eyes and she would marvel at the way the gray of his irises would change in the glow of candlelight.

One of Quinn's hands settled on her opposite hip, then slid slowly north, cupping her breast. When his thumb brushed over one nipple, she arched into the exciting caress. He rubbed her nipple in little teasing motions before gently squeezing. She moaned against his lips and flicked her tongue against his.

"My brave, bold lass." He nuzzled her cheek, their faces touching nose to nose before he slid down her body to where his face was level with her breasts.

When he closed his lips around one sensitive peak, she sucked in a breath and tugged at his hair. The sensation of him sucking at her made her body melt inside and wet heat pooled between her thighs. He moved to her other breast, lavishing the same attentions upon it before he slid back up her body and used one of his knees to part her legs. She had to make herself relax as he settled between her thighs.

He kissed her once more, sweetly, as he lifted his hips and she felt his hand between their bodies. Then he pushed into her, hard. The flash of pain was unexpected but still sharp enough that it stole her breath. Quinn lowered himself fully on top of her.

"Easy," he whispered in her ear. He nipped the lobe and she shivered, her inner walls tightening around him. He groaned in response.

"Did I hurt you?" she asked in a frantic whisper.

Quinn choked. "No, it feels good. *You* feel good." He smiled and kissed her.

The passion between them flared anew and she let go of the pain and her fears and gave herself over to the moment. She only noticed that he had started to move again when her body began to hum with pleasure. His shaft stretched her, almost too tight, but when he withdrew, she wrapped her arms around his hips, urging him to thrust back in. He was gentle at first, but the more she raised her hips, the deeper he sank into her and the quicker he moved. Finally he began to pound into her and she threw her head back, stars dotting her vision as he claimed her completely. The harsh sound of their breaths, the slide and smack of skin, and the burst of glorious pleasure could have lasted forever. When it finally faded, Rowena sank back down onto the bed with a weary sigh. Her body was limp and loose. Quinn lay above her, like a heavy warm masculine blanket. Their breath mingled and their bodies were still fused together.

Heaven...being with Quinn had been an exquisite heaven she never could have thought existed.

"That was wonderful, Quinn, more wonderful than I could have ever imagined. Was it good for you too?" She brushed the backs of her fingers over his cheek. His lashes fluttered as he opened his eyes.

"'Twas wonderful," he agreed solemnly.

He held on to her, his hands firm and tight as though she might vanish, but she wasn't going to; she wanted to stay right here with him. Finally he lifted his head. When their gazes met, an anxious knot formed in Rowena's stomach. Pain and hollowness were flashing in his eyes, like a lighthouse waving ships away from the shore.

"Quinn, what's the matter?" She hated how her eyes burned with traitorous tears, but she knew something was wrong.

Her husband rolled off her and sat up on the side of the bed, burying his head in his hands, his shoulders slumped.

"You'd best get some sleep." He reached behind him and flung a blanket toward her.

Startled, Rowena caught it and covered her suddenly chilly body.

Quinn stood and retrieved his smallclothes from the floor and put them on before he turned back to the bed. His focus was anywhere but on her as he extinguished the gas lamps and helped her under the blankets.

The bed was too small for them not to touch, and Rowena had to curl against him. As darkness settled around them, she felt tears rise in her eyes. Grateful he could not see, she buried her face in the softness of her pillow, soaking it with tears. She couldn't let him know how much he'd hurt her by his sudden emotional distance. The stress and exhaustion from the day finally caught up with her and she surrendered to sleep, praying tomorrow would be a better day.

Quinn held his breath as he listened to Rowena cry herself to sleep. He felt the little tremors of her body and with the barest hint of moonlight from their room's one window, he'd seen the tempting curve of one bare, feminine shoulder as it trembled.

She'd been charming, sweet, and all too seductive tonight. It was everything he loved in a woman, but after Maura had died, he'd vowed he wouldn't allow himself to feel that way again. He could enjoy sex, but he didn't want to fall in love and feel that pure sense of wonder at being connected so intimately with another person. His one joy in life aside from Blair was gone. He wasn't allowed a second chance. Life was not so forgiving as that.

Hours later he was still awake when Rowena shifted in her sleep, a soft little whimper escaping her. The pitiful sound tore at his heart. He reached for her purely on instinct and tucked her body so it fit into the protective curve of his own. Her muscles relaxed and she sighed, rolling over to face him as she did so. The silken tendrils of her hair caressed one of his arms, enticing with its softness.

His heart was torn in half. One part of him wished that the woman in his arms were someone else, the one he'd lost. The other half of him knew he was warming up to this young Englishwoman who'd been brave enough to leave her world behind for his.

She was so unlike Maura. She was short where Maura had been tall, her hair light like Blair's, whereas Maura's had been a dark red-gold. They did have one thing in common, though. They were both brave.

Quinn could still see Maura's pale face, tight with pain. The way she'd clutched his hand, the candles at her bedside fluttering in the dark as she struggled to breathe. Her last words were burned like a branding iron's mark upon his soul.

"I'm sorry, Quinn." For leaving him and Blair alone. As she'd drawn her last breath, his heart had turned to stone. It was the only way to stop the bleeding he'd felt inside. It was as though the part of Maura he'd held in his heart had been cut out. The pain too great, his loss too deep.

And here I am, with another. Not once during the moment of passion he'd shared with Rowena had he thought of Maura. Had he betrayed her memory? The question went unanswered and it continued to echo inside him. He prayed that marrying Rowena was not a mistake. If it was, it was too late to undo. But how was he to go on? He needed to keep his distance. He could not let himself be lost to passion, not again, because if he did, he might come to love her. And if he lost her to illness or childbirth too...

Quinn shuddered, and it made Rowena stir restlessly beside him. It was going to be a long night.

Chapter Eight

Rowena knew the next morning that what little ground she'd gained in the battle for Quinn's heart had been lost. Whatever he'd felt last night after their lovemaking, that mixture of melancholy and distance had returned. She'd woken to him already awake and dressed. He packed their bags with barely a word, and when a light breakfast was brought up, he did not even smile at her when she tried to smile at him.

Dressing in almost complete silence, she merely had to turn her back to him once and say his name in order for him to lace up her corset. He was quick and efficient this time, not like last night when he'd been gentle, slow, and seductive as he'd pulled the laces loose. He did not linger in his caresses or his attentions. She ate quickly and followed him to the waiting car, where a young man had loaded their luggage while she tried to ignore the ache in her chest.

What am I to do? Should I try to act normal? Yes, that would be best. He mustn't see how much I am hurting.

"How long is the drive to Forres?" she asked as she tugged the heavy wool coat around her shoulders.

"Half a day. We should arrive there by early afternoon." Quinn started the car and they were once more driving down the road.

Rowena gave up on conversation quickly. It was obvious from Quinn's monosyllabic responses he didn't wish to talk. She retrieved a book from her handbag, one of the few possessions she'd carried away from Pepperwirth Vale, and tried to read. She had been raised, along with Milly, to love reading, and normally it was easy to fall into a story's narrative and become lost to the world. But not this day. The silence seemed ominous between them, growing only stronger as they sat inches apart in the car, and Rowena found that for the first time in a long time, she could not read a single word.

They made one stop in a tiny Scottish village a short way from Forres to refuel before finishing the journey home.

"Quinn, do you mind if I stretch my legs a bit?" Rowena asked.

Her husband made a gruff noise she took for acceptance. Tugging her coat tight and fluffing the fur stole around her neck, she wandered up the snow-covered streets of the tiny village. Snow crunched beneath her boots, and the weight of heavy clouds pressed down upon her. Her breath came out in soft white clouds that faded seconds later. Rowena followed the street up, pausing to admire hats in a shop window. She looked over her shoulder at Quinn, who was entering a tavern to get hot drinks.

The cold tugged at the long locks of her hair and nipped at her cheeks. Rowena hurried farther up the street until she came across a silversmith's shop. Oil lamps lit the windows and an older woman with silver threaded through her light blond hair was polishing a set of spoons until sunlight glinted off them. She glanced up and saw Rowena, then waved her inside.

A small brass bell tinkled overhead as Rowena slipped inside the shop. The lamplight shined from the reflection of a dozen teapots and serving dishes.

"Escaping from the cold?" The woman's brown eyes sparkled with warmth.

"Oh yes. My husband and I are driving through and we stopped to stretch our legs."

"Newly married?" the woman guessed.

Flushing, Rowena nodded. "How could you tell?"

The shopkeeper chuckled and tapped her nose. "You have that fresh bride look, a little nervous, a little excited.

Marriage lasts a long time, lassie; 'tis not a race but a journey. You will settle in."

Rowena smiled, relaxing. "It isn't at all what I expected," she admitted.

The older woman's eyes sharpened. "He's not rough with you, is he?"

"No!" She waved her hands. "It's that...well, he doesn't love me. There was another, his first wife. She passed away a year ago. I thought, foolishly, I could win him over. I want to make him happy." It was not the sort of thing she should confess to a stranger, but Rowena had never been good at hiding her heart. Milly used to tease her, saying she wore it pinned to her gown sleeve.

"What is your husband like?" The woman bustled around the counter, which contained several rings and a collection of small knives and watches. "Maybe you could get him a wee gift? Men do like a present now and then, just like us."

"He's very serious." Rowena considered as she stepped closer to the glass counter, peering down at the items resting on a black velvet cloth.

"A serious man," the woman mused. "What family does he hail from?"

"He hails from Forres, but his family name is MacCauley." Rowena rested her head in one hand as she studied the set of daggers.

"MacCauley?" The woman across from her looked

startled. "You mean to say you're newly married to Quinn MacCauley?"

"Why, yes." Her heart skipped a few beats. Did this shopkeeper know her husband?

"I know just the thing. Wait here." The woman spun around and disappeared behind a blue curtain at the back of the shop. When she came back a moment later, she had something wrapped up in a slip of purple cloth. She set it on the counter and unrolled it. A slim dagger with a blade made of deer antler bone lay there. The blade had a crest carved into it. A pair of stag heads facing each other over a trio of stars.

"That is the MacCauley family crest."

"His family's?" Rowena marveled at the blade. "How can you be sure?"

The woman laughed. "Nigh on ten years ago, my husband won that in a game of cards from the late Earl of Forres. That'd be Quinn's father. He was a good man. I believe he let my Angus win. We were in need of coin that winter, like many folk here. The entire village was having a bad time of things. The old earl came through town and lost quite of bit of coin at the tavern that night during card games to men who needed it most for their families." The woman flashed Rowena a knowing smile as it dawned on her what the woman was saying. Quinn's father had lost the money on purpose to help the men feed and clothe their families. It had likely been more welcome than if the late earl had tried to give them charity.

"And the dagger? Your husband didn't sell it?"

"Ack, no. Angus knew what the earl meant by it and was so honored, he kept it. He always meant to find a way to return it. Then my Angus took ill last year and passed. God bless him." She pushed the dagger toward Rowena. "Take it, lassie. Give it to your husband."

Rowena opened her coat to search for her coin purse, but the woman scoffed.

"Now, now, none of that. I want only to know it gets back to the man it belongs to." There was a gleam in the older woman's eyes as she leaned over the counter to speak in a hushed tone. Rowena leaned in too.

"And if I were you, lassie, when you give him that present, it might be good to be wearing a lot less clothes, if you take my meaning. Men forget to keep their distance when a bonnie lassie is waiting for them in bed." With a wink, she shoved Rowena back out into the streets.

Clasping the dagger, Rowena wrapped it back up in the cloth and slid it into one of her coat pockets before walking to the motorcar. Quinn stood there, leaning against the door, his coat open and flapping slowly in the winter wind. His arms were crossed, and he was frowning slightly until he saw her. There was a flash of light in his serious eyes, a heat, a pleasure, before he banished it. That hint was all Rowena needed to summon her courage. She hastened her steps and when she reached him, she curled her arms around his neck and kissed him. Startled, he didn't immediately respond, but after a moment, he kissed her deeply, fire burning between their lips, his arms wrapping around her body to lift her up against him. After a long, delicious moment of kissing, he gently set her on her feet again. His cheeks were ruddy as he cleared his throat.

"Ready to go?"

"Yes." She smiled happily. There was still hope. Tonight she would do as the silversmith had said. She'd present Quinn with his father's dagger, and she'd do it in such a way he would want to take her back to bed.

The next hour passed quicker than Rowena expected. She spent the entire time quivering inside with excitement. She had a plan to win him over tonight. It would work; it had to.

"There it is, Castle Forres." Quinn's deep voice cut through the flash of giddy thoughts she was having.

Rowena focused on the view through her side of the car. In the distance, vast hills formed a ragged line against the sky. Closer still lay a gray stone house. It wasn't really a castle. It was more modern than medieval. Gothic peaked spires appeared through the heavy mists that had gathered as the day warmed. It made the castle appear like a crouched wolfhound, protective, a force to be reckoned with. The snow-covered lawns leading up to the front entrance were bare, but beyond the castle she saw the promise of a snow-veiled garden. It appeared harsh, but Rowena had a feeling it was like Quinn: a gruff serious exterior that would open up to reveal a soft heart.

When they reached the front door, Quinn parked the motorcar and got out. Rowena started to open her door, but he beat her to it and helped her out. It felt so wonderful to be in his arms again as he lowered her to the ground. She felt a little foolish, too, but she was a married woman now and enjoying her husband was her right, wasn't it?

The castle's tall oak door opened and a burly man in a black suit stood there, grim-faced and scowling slightly. Rowena mustered a smile as she and Quinn walked up to him. He stood back to allow them in.

"Welcome home, milord." He flicked his eyes over Rowena, the gaze sharp and cold. "Milady," he added as an afterthought.

Perhaps he's just a bit serious. She hoped that was the reason. She hated to think the butler disapproved of her only seconds after meeting her.

"Afternoon, Morris." Quinn nodded at the stiff butler. "This is Rowena, the new Countess of Forres. Rowena, this is Malcom Morris."

"Good afternoon," Rowena greeted, giving him what her father always said was her most winning smile.

The man did not blink once. His dark eyes were as cold as a frozen lake at midnight.

"Ah, here's the rest of the staff." Quinn brought Rowena farther into the house and announced a row of maids and footmen, but Rowena was only half listening. The housekeeper, Mrs. Stuart, was clutching a set of keys and frowning, much as Mr. Morris had done, as though upset that Rowena was here.

An anxious knot grew in the pit of her belly.

Am I so awful that they won't smile?

She knew, as any proper English lady of good breeding did, that a clear line existed between the occupants of the upper stairs and lower stairs, but she knew, too, that a smile upon greeting was not frowned upon. Perhaps Quinn's servants were afraid to meet her and therefore they were acting unusually formal.

"You all may go. Morris, where is my sister and the bairn?"

"They are in the nursery," the butler replied. "The child has had a bit of a cold the last few days."

"Oh?" Quinn paused, worry tightening his eyes.

"Aye, the good doctor was just here a few hours ago. He'll return tomorrow morning to see how the bairn feels," Morris replied, seemingly not that concerned. Children did often catch illnesses, but Rowena would do what she could to help Blair feel better.

"Thank you, Morris. Have the doctor see me first thing when he arrives tomorrow." Quinn handed his coat to the remaining footman and finally glanced at her.

"Well, take off your coat and I'll show you to the rooms I've had prepared."

"Oh, but—"

He halted on his way to the stairs after stammering a response. "Y-yes?"

"Might we see Blair first? I've missed her and it would do me good to hold her."

"It would?" Quinn's eyes widened.

Rowena nodded as she struggled out of her fur stole and coat, which the footman took from her. She didn't want to mention her feeling nervous about Blair suffering a cold; it would seem silly. Besides, the truth was that she missed Blair terribly. The little child had crawled into her heart alongside Quinn. Right now, she needed to cuddle the sick child and feel that she had at least one person who liked her.

"Yes, may we please see her?" She caught up with him on the stairs and captured his arm.

His gaze softened. "Of course. This way." He allowed her to loop her arm in his and the little victory filled her with quiet joy. Yet she couldn't help but wonder how many steps forward she could take before she would be dragged back.

I will win him. I must. If she couldn't, she'd face a life with a loveless marriage. A life without love was not a life worth living.

Quinn led Rowena down a dark paneled hallway. There were tall windows framed with evergreen curtains that when caught in the sunlight seemed to glow like the leaves of trees in the middle of summer. Maura had loved green, and summer had been her favorite time of year. She'd explore the hills and glens around Forres for hours on horseback. It was something they'd done together many times.

He couldn't help but wonder, what did Rowena prefer? The heat of summer or the promise of spring? Perhaps the beauty of winter or the breathtaking golds and reds of autumn? He dropped his gaze to the top of Rowena's head, momentarily bewitched by the way the afternoon light made the coiled coiffure of her blond locks glow like a delicate pile of spun gold.

Lord, he wanted to touch it, to tease the pins out of her hair and let the strands tumble down her shoulders in endless waves of brilliant sunny color. Quinn forced himself to remember his promise to keep his distance. He couldn't let Rowena's irresistible nature draw him in and tempt him to surrender to passion.

"Is the nursery very far from our room?" Rowena

lifted her head and met his gaze, calling him out of the lulling thoughts of her hair and how he wanted to kiss her.

"Aye, 'tis at the opposite side of the house."

"What?" She stopped short and stared at him. "Why would you put your daughter so far away from us?"

He didn't miss the word *us*. From the moment she'd met his child, she'd taken an interest in Blair. Yet her near-instant affection for his daughter always startled him. Rowena was young, barely old enough to start having bairns of her own, yet she wanted to care for a child who wasn't hers.

"The nursery has always been in the east wing."

Rowena's brow furrowed. "Well, I would like her moved closer to us. May we do that?"

Her delicate fingers curled around his arm and tightened their hold.

"Well." He paused, considering. It was normal to keep children out of the way...but he'd always wanted Blair close. Why hadn't it occurred to *him* to move her to a room closer to his?

"Please," she whispered. Rowena's eyes, those lovely cornflower blue eyes, were soft and pleading.

"If you wish it, then we can have the staff begin moving her to a room in our hallway."

"Thank you." Rowena was up on tiptoe, kissing his cheek, but he turned his face, catching her mouth with his. Her lips were soft and warm. The light brush of them sent bolts of arousal through him. He shut his eyes tight, grasping at his control. *You've had her already, and you promised to restrain yourself.*

"Rowena—" he murmured, beginning to lose himself in her touch, her kiss.

"Quinn! You're back!" His sister's voice startled him and he stepped back from Rowena. Kenna stood at the end of the hallway, holding Blair's hand.

"Kenna." He ushered Rowena forward. His wife glanced at him, her cheeks pink and then she looked away.

"Rowena, this is my sister, Kenna. Kenna, this is Rowena."

Kenna's eyes leapt from his face to his wife's, a curious gleam there. Then she held out a hand to Rowena, who grasped it.

"Welcome to Forres." Kenna smiled and glanced down at Blair. "Blair, love, say hello to Rowena."

The little girl buried her face in Kenna's skirts as though shy too. She swayed, her little black dress with a white pinafore waving like a bell in a church steeple. When she glanced at him, Quinn smiled and winked indulgently. Every time he looked at his child, his heart filled with a quiet joy. He noticed her cheeks were a tad too pink and her nose a little red. So she had been feeling a little unwell. It was good the doctor would return on the morrow.

Rowena let go of his arm and knelt on the ground,

arms outstretched. “Do you remember me, Blair? We looked at lily pads in the garden together.”

Blair peeped out from the folds of Kenna’s skirts and gave a tiny nod. “We looked for fishes.” She had such a tiny, high-pitched little voice, like a wee bird chattering. It made his chest ache when Blair spoke.

“That’s right, we did.” Rowena grinned. “May I have a hug, Blair? I’m awfully lonely and it would make me feel better.” Rowena curled her fingers in invitation, and Blair, as though mesmerized, released Kenna’s skirts and ambled forward to tuck herself into Rowena’s arms.

It was impossible to miss the relief and joy in Rowena’s face the moment she picked Blair up and cuddled her close. Rowena began to speak softly to the child, telling her about the long car journey and how excited she was to come to live here. Blair stared at her, one thumb tucked in her mouth, as she listened with rapt attention.

The two of them walked down the hall, giving Quinn a minute alone with his sister.

“She’s very pretty, Quinn. You didn’t tell me that.” Kenna was watching him, her too-observant gaze pinning him to the floor.

“She is, but it doesn’t matter. I did not marry her because she is pretty. I married her so Blair can have a mother and to help you, so you do not have to stay here and run the house.”

His sister crossed her arms over her chest. “If you

think you're going to stay away from a lovely lass like that, you're a damned fool, brother."

Quinn curled his hands into fists. "Kenna, I don't love her, and she isn't here for me but for my child. That is all." The words came out louder than he'd intended, and it was then he heard the silence. Rowena and Blair were staring at him from the end of the hallway. Rowena's eyes were bright with tears.

She bit her lip and glanced at Blair. "Which room is the nursery? I'd like to take her back so she can play. And then if it's not too much trouble, I'd like some tea." She spoke not to him, but instead to Kenna.

"Of course. I was just about to have the nurse ring for a maid to bring me a fresh pot. This way."

His sister sent him a quelling gaze that threatened him pain if he dared to come after them. As they entered the nursery a few doors away, he stood there, feeling like a fool and a bloody bastard. He should not have said what he did, especially not when Rowena stood so close. Still, she needed to know what his intentions were. This was a marriage of convenience, not a love match. The sooner she learned that, the better off she would be.

Chapter Nine

Blair squirmed as Rowena set her down inside the nursery. The old nurse was seated in an armchair in the corner by a fire, snoring. Rowena and Kenna shared a look before both of them stifled giggles.

"She's a dear, I promise, but she was Quinn's and mine and we're all grown now. Quinn didn't have the heart to replace her."

"It means we need to watch Blair more carefully. When I first met her, she was on the verge of falling face-first into a fountain, and now she's got a cold." Rowena gazed at the little girl, who toddled over to the rug by the fire, playing with a pair of well-loved dolls. The child half hummed, half sang a little song as she played.

"Children do get colds now and then," Kenna chuckled. “Ian, I mean Dr. McIntosh, came to check on her today. He’ll be back tomorrow.”

Rowena stared at Blair’s rosy cheeks, still worried. But the child was amusing herself and seemed quite fine.

“You really like her, don’t you,” Kenna mused.

“Hmm?” Rowena was pulled from her daydreams of Blair playing with another child, one a little younger, with her eyes and Quinn’s dark hair.

“I can see it in the way you look at her.” Kenna leaned back in her chair and studied Rowena.

The intense scrutiny made her flinch. “Yes, I do. I suppose it sounds silly but the moment I held her in my arms, it felt like she belonged to me.”

If only her father belonged to me too… Quinn’s biting words still lingered inside her, cutting her up into little painful pieces. *“I don’t love her.”*

“Why did you agree to marry my brother?”

Kenna’s blunt question caught her off guard.

“I…” Heat rushed to her face and she dropped her gaze.

“I suppose he is handsome,” Kenna continued. “But you don’t seem to be the sort of woman who is swayed merely by a man’s looks.”

Emboldened by Kenna’s friendliness, Rowena decided honesty was best. “Quinn is handsome, very handsome, but…” She paused, considering her words. “I was drawn to him because of his smile. He does it so rarely, and when he told me about his wife and Blair, my heart opened up to him, to them both. I want to heal him. It sounds silly," she added.

Kenna reached out and covered her hands. "No, it doesn't." Quinn's sister's gaze was level. "My mother used to say that some souls were marked for each other. Branded in a way. Like you were born to be with someone. Mated souls, you understand."

Mated souls? The notion was a tad romantic, but Rowena liked to think of such things. Milly had always been more sensible than her, but Rowena loved the idea of love and destiny.

"And I suppose you mean to tell me Quinn and his first wife were...mated souls?"

Kenna shrugged. "I do not know, except that he and Maura were happy. What I do know is my brother and how he behaves. He would not have married you if he did not care for you, no matter what silly things you hear him say. There is a vast difference between not loving someone and *not wanting* to love someone. No doubt my foolish brother has convinced himself that loving another woman betrays Maura's memory somehow. I wouldn't worry about it. I suspect he'll succumb to your sweetness before long." Kenna said this teasingly, but she had no idea how much Rowena wished it to be true.

Playing with the folds of her skirt, Rowena sighed

heavily. "I want so much to win his heart, but he doesn't want me."

Kenna chuckled. "You make him out to be a saint. My brother wouldn't be so selfless. If he married you, there is a reason and it is not just for Blair's sake. He's just too damned thickheaded to admit it."

Hope blossomed inside Rowena. "Do you really think so?"

"I do. The question is, are you brave enough to put him to the test?"

She couldn't help but remember Quinn murmuring in the darkness, *"My bold, brave lass."*

"I can be brave."

"Good. Then we will find a way to get you alone with him as much as possible. My mother used to say when a man is tempted by a pretty ankle, he'll come around." It echoed what Rowena had heard in the shop in the village.

"But how—"

"And you ought to demand your marital rights every night. Keep him busy in your bed and the man will not be missing anyone else."

Rowena bit her lip and glanced away, embarrassment heating her face.

Good heavens, these Scots aren't afraid to speak so frankly of such personal matters.

"I suppose I could try..."

"I know, we ought to have a fancy dinner tonight. You

can wear your best dress. We rarely do it here, so we might as well take the chance when we have it. I'll mention it to Quinn."

"I don't suppose we could invite anyone to join us? Neighbors or friends?" Rowena prayed there were some people close by or else the dinner with just the three of them might prove to be awkward.

Kenna curled her hand into a fist and rested her chin atop it. "Well, not so much. We're a way off from town and few like to travel in the winter. But never you mind." She patted Rowena's hand. "Let me go wake the nurse to watch Blair and I'll take you to your chambers."

After they'd left the nurse in charge of the babe, Rowena followed Kenna, trying to memorize her way through the maze of corridors.

"Quinn always keeps his chambers in the west wing. Before Maura died, they had chambers in the north part of the house, but we rarely go there these days. Ah, here we are." She stopped in front of a door and opened it.

The room was bright and cheery with butter-yellow walls and high ceilings. A red marble fireplace was on the right side of the room and on the wall closest to Rowena sat a tall Chippendale carved canopy bed with blue silk hangings. Cornflower blue. Like her eyes.

"I see the footmen have brought your bags. I'll leave you to settle in. Pull this"—Kenna touched a silk cord by the door—"if you need anything."

Rowena touched her shoulder before the other woman could leave. "Kenna, thank you. You've made me feel better. I was so..." She floundered for words, but Kenna held up her hand.

"I can see how much you love my brother. It's all over your face. How could I not love a woman who loves him as you do?" Kenna leaned forward and embraced her, a light but intimate hug, as though they'd become sisters in such a short time. It reminded Rowena of how much she missed Milly. In the span of two days, it was as though she'd lived a lifetime, and there was so much she wished to share with her sister. But she couldn't. They were no longer sleeping down the hall from one another. They were married and living hundreds of miles apart.

Rowena sat on the bed and sighed. It had been an awfully long day. All she wanted now was a warm fire and a pot of hot tea. She reached for the bell cord and pulled on it. Soon enough a servant would come and she could make her requests. Until then, she could catch a tiny bit of rest. She curled up on the bed, tucking her skirts underneath her, and let her head drop onto the pillow. It would only be for a moment...

Quinn had spent the entire afternoon talking with Morris and sorting out arrangements for Rowena to take over much of the day-to-day decisions at the house. It would leave him free to spend more time on the grounds around the castle. Much of the estate's upkeep came from outdoor renovations, keeping the wild game under control and the like.

He was finishing up with Morris when his sister strolled into the study. Notions of privacy, or even the consideration of knocking, had never been Kenna's strong suit.

"Quinn, you ought to have a lovely dinner tonight to celebrate your and Rowena's wedding. Don't you agree?" She settled herself in a chair opposite his large desk and played with her skirts.

"Well..."

"You didn't celebrate in England, but you ought to here, don't you think?" Kenna pressed.

He leaned forward and rested his elbows on his desk. "What are you up to, Kenna?"

"Up to? I'm not up to anything. Rowena's a lovely lass and I simply think a formal dinner would be best." His sister's gray eyes were wide and innocent, but he knew she was scheming. Perhaps it wouldn't hurt to play along.

"If you desire it, then why not go tell the kitchens to prepare it for this evening."

I can suffer one dinner and not be distracted by Rowena and how much I want to take her to bed, can't I?

He didn't like that he couldn't seem to find the answer to that question. All afternoon she'd been on his mind. The sight of her tears, the feel of her lips on his, the soft, silky tendrils of her hair. He hadn't wanted to hurt her, but it would only be cruel to pretend there was something more between them, at least for him.

"I'll go speak to the cook. See you this evening." Kenna stood and was halfway out the door when she paused, her fingertips tapping on the door frame. She glanced over her shoulder at him.

"You aren't the only one who misses Maura, you know. She wasn't the sort of person who would want you to be unhappy. Find your joy again, Quinn." She tapped the frame once more and vanished from view.

Quinn rested his elbows on his desk and covered his face with his hands, suddenly weary. Kenna was right. He'd been too cruel today to Rowena in his attempt to keep his distance. Standing, he walked around the edge of his desk and rested his hands on his hips, debating.

I should apologize. That would be the right thing to do.

It took him half an hour to find Rowena. None of the servants seemed to know where she was. By the time he thought to check her bedchamber, he was startled to find her asleep on the bed, her body shivering. No fire had been lit and no tea brought to her...He gave a mighty tug on the servant's bell cord by her bed and waited. For a long while nothing happened. No maid came rushing to the door. With a little growl, he tugged the cord again. It was clear no one was coming. A problem he would deal with later. He checked the time on the clock above her fireplace. It was an hour until dinner would be served.

Quinn approached the bed, his hands itching with the urge to touch her. The invisible pull she had on him was unsettling. What made this young English woman so irresistible? She was undeniably pretty, but looks hadn't mattered to him before, not as much as other things anyway.

"Rowena, wake up." He surrendered to the temptation to touch her and gave her a light kiss on the cheek.

When she still didn't stir, he gave her shoulder a delicate shake. She sighed, rolled onto her back, and exposed the swanlike curve of her neck and the soft swells of her full breasts covered by the gown she wore.

"Five more minutes, Milly," she murmured sleepily. "I'm having the most wonderful dream." She wriggled her body and smiled, her eyes still closed.

Fascinated, Quinn leaned over and whispered in her ear, "What are you dreaming about, lassie?"

In response, her nose wrinkled and she sighed again. "The most wonderful man. He wants me to dance..."

Dance? He'd not yet danced with her, which meant she might be dreaming of someone else. That thought brought him up sharply. She was his wife, and while he had vowed not to love her, he was not going to let her fall in love with another man, even in her dreams.

Quinn bent and pressed a kiss to her lips. She tasted sweet, too sweet. It made him think of Christmases when he'd been a lad and he'd eaten candied chestnuts by the fire and Kenna crawled around on blankets, playing with toy dolls.

The kiss deepened as Rowena responded, her arms coming up to curl around his neck. For such an innocent creature, she knew how to kiss. It was something that came naturally to women. Men had to learn.

"Heaven," Rowena signed as his lips moved to her cheek, then along her jaw and down to her throat. She made a little purr of pleasure that sent a bolt of arousal straight to his groin. He could get lost in her kisses. She gave him a whole heart when she came alive like this.

"Quinn," she moaned his name, and he froze. Her mouth teased his a moment longer before her dark brown lashes fluttered up. He was still leaning over her, she still clutching him in an embrace, yet neither of them seemed to know what to say.

"Quinn, I'm so glad to see you." The genuine joy in her smile tore at his heart.

Clearing his throat, he sat down on the bed beside her. He knew he should keep his distance, but he didn't want to, at least not now that he'd stopped kissing her.

"Why is there no fire lit in your room? And why has no one brought you tea?"

She glanced down, her cheeks turning a bright pink. "I don't know. I rang for the maid but...and then I was so tired and no one came..."

He didn't like the idea of her staying in a room that did not have a working cord.

"You're freezing, love. Why not come over to my rooms for a while to warm up. Dinner is in an hour."

Rowena nodded. "Could I take a bath? It might warm me up before we eat." She nibbled her bottom lip in a way that was fast becoming a huge distraction for him.

"Er...yes. You may use mine." It would be warmer there. That was the lie he told himself as he curled an arm around her waist, led her to the door, and walked her down the hall.

"Our rooms are not connected?" She raised her brows, and he saw that all-too-familiar gleam of pain in them.

"Not yet. The only connected rooms were in another wing. I plan to renovate in the spring." It was a lie. He'd had no intention of connecting their rooms, because there would be no need. He hadn't planned on visiting her bed that frequently.

"Do you..." She halted outside his room and glanced about as though afraid to be overheard.

"Yes?" he prompted, leaning down a little, bringing

their faces close. It was impossible not to look at her lips when he was mere inches from them.

"Well, it's just that I should like to be with you, Quinn. It would be silly to have one of us running up and down the hall. Could I stay in your room with you or do you think the servants would find it too scandalous?" She gazed up at him and he knew in that moment he was lost. There was nothing she could have asked for that he would deny her. Not when she gazed at him like that, as though he were her hero.

"If you wish to, then I suppose you can. The downstairs will be in an uproar, of course, but we can weather the scandal if necessary." He smiled despite himself. It was a terrible idea to let her share his bed, but he couldn't say no.

As much as he wished it weren't true, he *wanted* to hold her deep into the night. It was one of the things he had dearly missed as a widower. There was no woman who belonged to him, no woman who he could tuck into his side and sleep with. Surely it would not be a bad thing to let himself have this one little joy in life.

We will sleep, nothing more. I hope. Even as he thought this, his mind replayed their wedding night, how wonderful it felt to have her beneath him, to taste her lips, to feel her body grip him tightly as they chased the building waves of pleasure.

"Thank you, Quinn." Rowena was kissing him again and he lost control in a mere instant.

He rotated their bodies and pinned her against the wall, his hands exploring her curves, shaping the flare of her hips and the softness of her breasts. She arched into him, nipping at his lips playfully. He loved that about her, how she made him feel young and happy again. Losing Maura had aged him a decade, but being with Rowena, and her teasing kisses and playful nibbles, resurrected the ghosts of his youthful passions.

Years of practice had him lifting her up and carrying her to his bedroom. They only bumped into one wall and it was his arm he knocked into the wood paneling. With a little curse at the pain, he finally reached the bed and dropped her onto it. The woman was giggling. Quinn climbed up the bed over her and his clever wife was already working at the buttons on his waistcoat and peeling it off his shoulders. When she reached for his trousers, he gently pushed her hands away so he could get them off faster. Desire fogged his head, and his lips curved into a boyish grin that couldn't be helped.

"You're so lovely," he whispered as he bent to kiss her. His hands rucked her skirts up to her thighs and he growled in frustration at all the fabric preventing him from reaching what he needed most.

Laughing, Rowena lifted her bottom so he could push the skirts to her waist. He covered one stocking-clad knee with his palm, urging her to part her legs as he tugged at her drawers. There was something wonderfully sinful about taking a woman fully clothed.

They shared a moan as he sank into her welcoming heat. She was damned tight, but wet and hot enough to burn him.

As he thrust into her deeper, their hips jerked together. She whimpered and threw her head back. Pins scattered as her blond hair broke free of the elaborate coiffure and rippled across the dark blue coverlet. Something inside him, a dark animal side, broke free. He didn't want to hold back, not any longer. He covered Rowena's mouth with his, kissing hard, giving her no chance to breathe as he drove into her again and again. He didn't want to think about how he desired her, about how being with her like this drove him mad with hunger. It was like nothing else he'd ever experienced. When he was inside her, he couldn't think past his next breath, the next surge back into her body, and how good it felt when she squeezed him with her inner muscles. His heart beat thunderously and boomed against his eardrums.

Her palms slid over his body, clawing at the shirt he still wore. They'd not gotten past his trousers and her undergarments. And he didn't care. He needed more...he needed...Panting, he lifted up off her and rolled her over onto her stomach, raising her dress over her bare bottom. He gripped her hips, repositioned himself, and thrust back into her from behind. Rowena hissed in surprise and dug into the blankets as she stifled a low moan.

That never-ending sense of madness and the need to connect to her kept pulsing through him and he rammed into her over and over.

He was aware, dimly, of her coming apart beneath him by the sounds of her muffled cries. Quinn didn't bother to do the same. He came with a shout and an exhalation as his body went limp. Doing his best to not crush her, he collapsed onto the bed and kept her tucked against him. Her bare bottom still rubbed against his groin and he moaned in lethargic pleasure.

Rowena was quiet, except for her shallow, quick breaths. His stomach clenched in sudden worry and he leaned over her, cupping her face to turn it toward his. Tears coated her lashes and her eyes were a little red.

"Rowena, lass, are you all right?" His voice roughened as his anxiety deepened. He'd hurt her? Been too rough? *Bloody barbarian, I am...*

"I'm fine," she whispered. "I...well...it was so intense. I didn't know..." Her cheeks were red as fresh cranberries.

"Aye, it can be intense." He paused, wondering how to explain what they'd experienced. He'd been married and in love before. He knew from experience that sex with someone you loved was overwhelming, not just physically but emotionally. If Rowena was feeling that way now, she was falling in with love with him. He'd known she would fall for him. She was too open, too young and sweet not to fall for her husband. And what truly worried him was how powerful his feelings for her had been, still were...

"Have I upset you?" She tried to smile, but her lips quivered. It made something deep inside him stir, like a bird in its nest after winter had passed. It was strange...he had not felt...what it was he could not readily identify.

"I'm not upset," he promised, and against his better judgment he bent his head to hers for a slow, lingering kiss that burned clear through him like shafts of winter sunlight piercing clouds.

"I forgot how young you are." He smiled. Ten years felt like a lifetime between them in moments like this.

Her face was still dark with uncertainty and yet he didn't know what to say to put her at ease.

"Why don't you take a bath before dinner. We'll eat soon."

He crawled off the bed and fixed his clothes. He'd need a bath, too, but it would be too tempting to join Rowena.

As soon as he escaped into the hall, he strode back to Rowena's chambers and tested the bell cord by her bed again. He waited patiently for several minutes and still no servant came. Her valise lay untouched, her clothes still inside. What the devil was wrong here? She should have been immediately taken care of, her clothes unpacked, tea and biscuits brought up, a maid to see to her bath...Anger roiled beneath his skin. Scowling, he left her chamber and stalked down the hall to the stairs leading to the servants' quarters.

"Morris!" he bellowed.

His butler peered out from his small office.

"My lord?"

Quinn waited, arms crossed as Morris walked toward him.

"Is there a reason my wife's bedchamber cord is not working? No one has come to light a fire. No one has brought her tea or helped her unpack. She was *freezing*, Morris. Explain that to me. The mistress of this house treated like she's invisible?"

All the color drained from Morris's face and he tugged at his collar, his gaze darting anywhere but at Quinn. As his butler stalled, several maids and footmen gathered in the hall to watch. Someone hissed, "Sassenach." Quinn met each of the watching servants' eyes before speaking again.

"I will not tolerate this treatment of my wife. I expect the bell cord to be repaired, and I expect all of you to go out of your way to treat your mistress with care and kindness, or else you will be tossed out on your ear without references. Is that clear?"

He did not like the idea of doing this to anyone on his staff, but in the few minutes he'd spent down here, he realized that his staff did not like Rowena for the simple reason she was English, and that infuriated him.

He left the servants' quarters, frowning as he went back upstairs to summon his gamekeeper. He planned to go deer stalking in a few days and needed to make arrangements. Hunting would give him time alone to think about his new wife and how she was getting under his skin...and coming perilously close to getting into his heart.

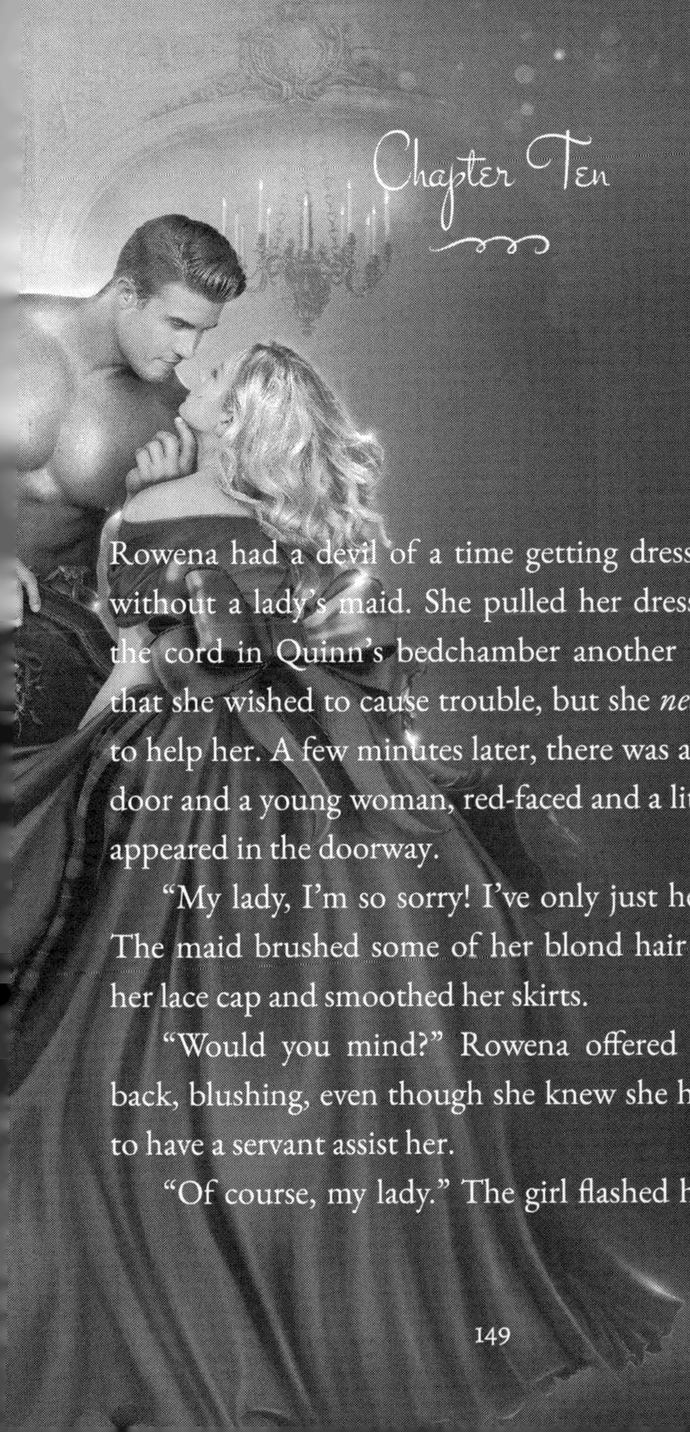

Chapter Ten

Rowena had a devil of a time getting dressed for dinner without a lady's maid. She pulled her dress up and gave the cord in Quinn's bedchamber another tug. It wasn't that she wished to cause trouble, but she *needed* someone to help her. A few minutes later, there was a knock on the door and a young woman, red-faced and a little breathless, appeared in the doorway.

"My lady, I'm so sorry! I've only just heard the bell." The maid brushed some of her blond hair back beneath her lace cap and smoothed her skirts.

"Would you mind?" Rowena offered the maid her back, blushing, even though she knew she had every right to have a servant assist her.

"Of course, my lady." The girl flashed her a shy smile

and started fastening up the hooks on the back of Rowena's gown.

"What's your name?" Rowena asked, and tugged up the front of her rose-pink silk dress. Turkish panels of silver gilt embroidery made the gown elegant and imperial but the soft silk showed off her figure by draping over her breasts and hips and gathered with a sash at her waist.

"I'm Gwen, your ladyship." She held out a pair of long, white elbow-length gloves.

"Thank you, Gwen." She slipped the gloves on, tugging them tight, and then she studied her appearance in the mirror critically. Her hair was...well, a bit wild. The locks were free and unbound after her bath.

"Shall I arrange your hair?"

"Oh yes, please." She seated herself at Quinn's small desk in the corner and handed the maid a comb and a few pins she'd kept from before her bath.

"If it would please you, my lady, I'd be happy to attend to you as your permanent lady's maid, unless you wish to send for someone else." Gwen offered this nervously.

Rowena smiled before she replied and remembered all too well how nervous she'd been coming to Forres. It would be nice to have someone to talk to. A lady's maid would be loyal to her and would be trustworthy.

"Thank you, Gwen. I would like that very much."

Once she was properly attended to, Rowena smiled at Gwen and made her way to the dining room. Kenna was waiting for her, wearing a lovely plum silk gown accented with black beaded embroidery on the bodice and hem.

"You look lovely!" Rowena embraced her sister-in-law.

"So do you." Kenna gave her hand a little squeeze. "Quinn is running late. Shouldn't be—"

"I'm here." Quinn strode into the dining room. He wore a tailless black dinner jacket and black trousers with a black tie. The coat molded to his frame, displaying that muscled figure she'd glimpsed undressed on only a few occasions.

Tonight I shall be with him again. She fretted with her gloves as he came toward her and Kenna. When he gave them both a gentle, chaste kiss, Rowena swallowed down the flutter of longing and disappointment.

Throughout dinner, Quinn and Kenna talked about friends they shared and old acquaintances, but Rowena didn't know them and could add little to the conversation. As the courses came and went, Rowena tasted only ash in her mouth. She'd been so excited to look nice for dinner, but after Quinn's almost brotherly kiss she feared tonight would not work out as she had hoped.

I'm an outsider. She hadn't wanted to face that realization and she'd been a fool to ignore it. Poking a fork around on her plate, she nudged the roast goose in an attempt to distract herself.

"Rowena?" Quinn's gentle voice rumbled her name and she glanced up.

She dropped her fork and it clinked sharply on the china. "Yes?"

"Blair was asking after you. If, after dinner, you wished to see her to bed..." The look of longing in his gray eyes startled her.

"I would love to." Bolstered by the beaming approval in his face, Rowena didn't mind that she felt so isolated. Blair wanted to see her.

After dessert, Kenna bid them good night and vanished up the stairs toward her chamber. Quinn took Rowena's arm in his and together they walked toward the hallway where their chambers were. But he stopped in front of a different door, one not far from his own. She looked at him in surprise as she realized he had done as she wished. Hope stirred weakly in her chest; she was afraid to give it more strength lest he destroy it again.

"You had her moved?"

"Aye. It was important to you to have her close." His face reddened as he glanced down, a little sheepish. The sweet behavior, almost boyish, was charming on such a rugged, handsome man. It softened the hard lines around his mouth and brightened his eyes.

Inside the bedchamber, the nurse was sitting by the fire, knitting what looked to be a rather lovely scarf. Blair was dressed in her nightclothes, tucked in blankets but by the fire and not in her bed.

"Papa!" Blair squealed, and ran to them.

Rowena's heart swelled at the sight of father and daughter as he embraced her with one large arm.

"Rowena is here to say good night to ye, lass." He brushed a hand over her curls and glanced at Rowena.

"Rowena," the little girl said solemnly, and held out a chubby hand.

Clutching Blair's hand, Rowena followed the child to her bed and then she lifted Blair up and nestled her beneath her covers.

"Are you warm enough?" she asked the little girl as she tucked the blankets up to her chin. Then she placed the back of one hand to Blair's forehead. The skin was still too hot and Blair's gray eyes were a little glassy. Rowena wanted to be there when the doctor examined the child and learn what she could about how to help Blair get better.

"Sing a song," Blair murmured drowsily, her cheeks pink with a smile that would have melted even the coldest hearts.

"A song?" Rowena tapped her chin, pretending to think it over.

"Pu-lease?" Blair whispered. "Mamas always sing songs."

Rowena's breath caught for a moment and she couldn't breathe. *Mama*. The word held an infinite amount of hope for Rowena. It was part of why she was here. She wanted to be a mother to this child and a wife and lover to Quinn. Could she truly be one step closer to her dreams of true happiness?

"You're right. Mamas do sing songs," Rowena agreed after a second. "This is one my mother used to sing to me." She began to hum the melody of "The Lost Chord" by Sir Arthur Sullivan.

"Seated one day at the organ, I was weary and ill at ease,

And my fingers wander'd idly over the noisy keys;

I know not what I was playing, or what I was dreaming then,

But I struck one chord of music like the sound of a great Amen.

It flooded the crimson twilight like the close of an Angel's Psalm,

And it lay on my fever'd spirit with a touch of infinite calm.

It quieted pain and sorrow like love overcoming strife,

It seem'd the harmonious echo from our discordant life.

It link'd all perplexed meanings into one perfect peace

And trembled away into silence as if it were loth to cease;

I have sought, but I seek it vainly, that one lost chord divine,

Which came from the soul of the organ and enter'd into mine."

As she finished part of the song, she noticed Blair's

eyes were closed, her lashes a dusting of gold across the tops of her cheeks.

"Good night, sleep well, darling." She curled the blankets around Blair's neck more tightly and then she turned around. Quinn wasn't there.

She glanced at the nurse, whose eyes were bright with tears. She wordlessly pointed at the open door, and Rowena rushed after him. She caught up with Quinn halfway down the corridor. The lamps had been dimmed in the evening and seeing his dark form seeming so remote from her sent shivers of fear through her stomach, making it cramp.

"Quinn? What's the matter?" Her whisper broke the thick silence of the corridor. She gripped his shoulder and jerked him to a halt.

Her husband fell back against the wall, his chest heaving as he sucked in breaths. When he finally raised his face, tears coursed down his cheeks, and his fists were clenched. He looked...broken. The stark pain and anguish in his features rent her soul in half.

"I *lied* to myself." His hoarse whisper broke her apart.

"Lied?" She echoed, her ears ringing. This should not be happening. They were supposed to be happy. They should have been laughing and smiling after tucking the child into bed and heading to their own with other things than sleep upon their minds. They weren't supposed to be...standing across a chasm in a darkened corridor, both their hearts breaking.

"Aye...I'm not ready. I can't..." He rubbed at his eyes, dispelling the evidence of his tears. Shaking, Rowena reached out to touch him but he jerked away.

"I'm...sorry. I don't understand." She curled her arms around herself, trying to keep her own sobs from escaping.

"I loved her. I loved her with every part of my heart. Yet being with you—for only a few days...I'm replacing her. Blair won't even remember Maura." He choked on the words before he could continue. "I can't help but feel like I'm erasing the memory of her by bringing you here."

There was no accusation in his tone, but the bleak despair of his words splintered inside Rowena's chest, making it near impossible to breathe. She never wanted to replace Quinn's first wife, but she'd wanted to claim this new life for herself with a husband and a child. Blair's little voice calling her Mama... *Am I destroying Maura's memory? But what about me? Am I not entitled to a happy life?* Confusion clouded her thoughts. What was she supposed to do when he was breaking her heart?

"Quinn..." His name stung her lips and she clamped them shut, eyes burning with tears. "Do you...do you want me to leave?" If he said yes, it would break her in a way nothing else ever would.

"Leave?" He whispered the word, his brows drawn

together in confusion. "We're married, Rowena. We've consummated our vows in bed."

"Then what is it you want me to do? I don't—" She stumbled on her words, hurt and frustrated almost beyond rationality.

"I don't know," he muttered, his eyes failing to meet hers. "I shouldn't have said anything. I just need time is all. I'm sorry, lass." He turned and strode away, leaving her in the dim hall. The tapestries on either side of her rustled with a faint draft and she couldn't stop it when her entire body began to shake violently. She walked numbly back to her own empty chambers. The sight of Gwen setting out nightclothes and a warm fire in the hearth was her only relief.

I must not cry.

"Miss, I found this in your coat as I was hanging it up." Gwen held out the dagger wrapped in velvet. The present she'd planned to give Quinn tonight. That was before everything had changed.

"Thank you, Gwen."

She held the dagger in her hands, remembering when she'd received it in the village. She'd had such wonderful dreams and hopes then about how she would give it to Quinn.

And he would love me...perhaps just a little more than before.

That hope was now tainted with regret and sorrow.

She considered hiding the dagger away or shoving it at him and running back to the safety of her own, empty chambers. But no grand gesture, negative or otherwise, would make her feel better.

I should give it to him and let it be the end.

"I'll only be a moment, Gwen." She returned to Quinn's bedchamber, relieved to find him gone. She dug around in his desk for paper and a pen before leaving him a note. It took her two tries to write it because tears kept blurring her vision, but finally she said what she needed to, sealed the letter, and left it with the dagger on his bed. Then she returned to her chamber. All dreams of being with him tonight or any other night were gone.

I was a fool to believe he would ever love me.

She changed into her nightclothes and crawled into bed, numb and wounded beyond repair. What was she going to do? She couldn't leave Blair, and she couldn't leave him, even if he was crushing her hopes of being a happy wife and mother.

"I just need time is all..."

How long would that be? Would she be sitting across from him for silent, awkward dinners for a decade before he decided to give her a chance? Rowena curled her hands into fists as she lay in her bed, sucking in shaky breaths.

I made a promise to myself and to him that I would heal him, that I would be the woman to bring him through his pain, but how can I do that when he shuts me out?

Her tears soaked through her pillow but she couldn't stop crying. The ghost of Maura had not left this house, nor had she left Quinn's heart. Rowena didn't want to replace Maura; she only ever wanted to share him.

An impossible dream that cost her a broken heart.

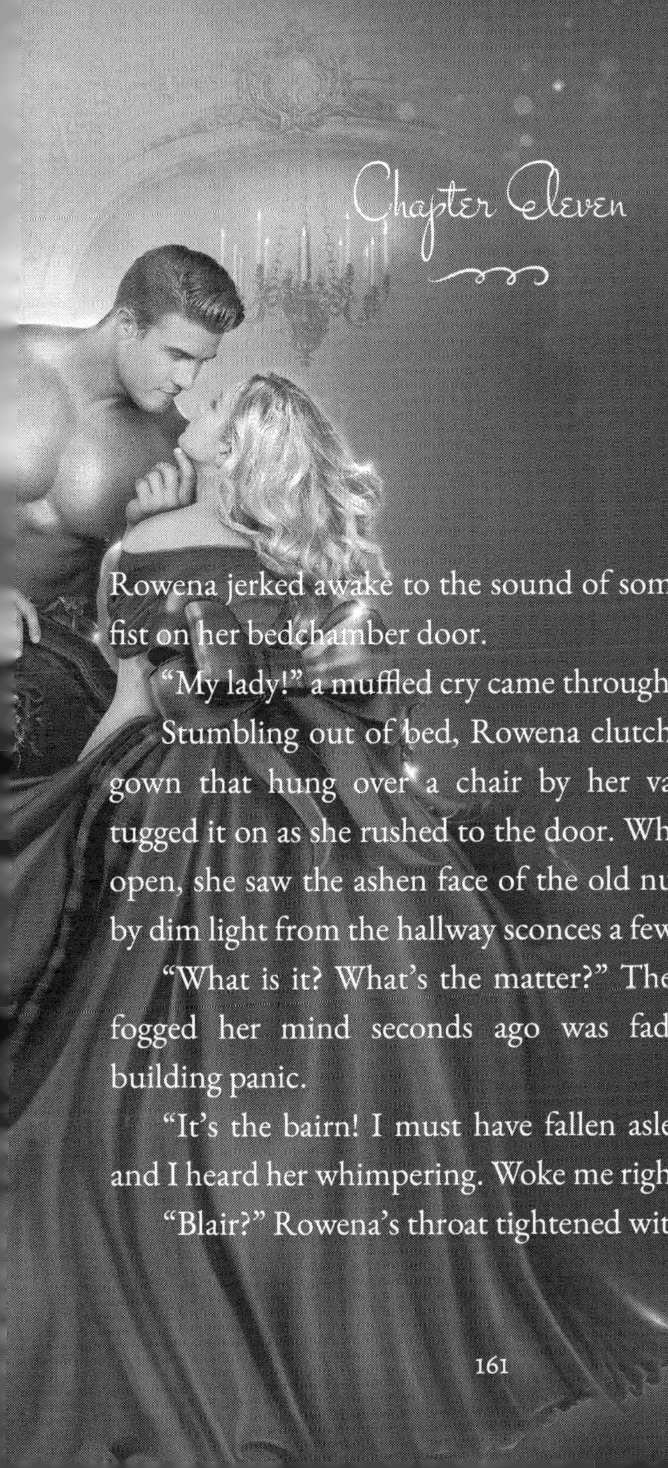

Chapter Eleven

Rowena jerked awake to the sound of someone banging a fist on her bedchamber door.

"My lady!" a muffled cry came through the wood.

Stumbling out of bed, Rowena clutched the dressing gown that hung over a chair by her vanity table and tugged it on as she rushed to the door. When she pulled it open, she saw the ashen face of the old nurse illuminated by dim light from the hallway sconces a few feet away.

"What is it? What's the matter?" The sleep that had fogged her mind seconds ago was fading under the building panic.

"It's the bairn! I must have fallen asleep in the chair and I heard her whimpering. Woke me right up."

"Blair?" Rowena's throat tightened with fear.

"Aye, she's worsened. The fever is too strong. I cannae wake her!" The nurse's face was stained with tears.

"No, oh no," Rowena murmured in a horrified daze. "Take me to her at once!" The nurse and Rowena rushed down the corridor and into Blair's room.

Quinn was there at the child's bed, holding her cradled in his lap as he sat on the edge of the small feather tick mattress. Blair looked impossibly small and frail in his large arms. Sweat-soaked strands of hair clung to the girl's forehead and neck. Rowena rushed over to them, kneeling in front of Quinn so she could see Blair better.

"Her breathing is too shallow." His hoarse whisper was choked with pain and Rowena's eyes stung with tears.

"You need to get Dr. McIntosh. I'll stay with her," Rowena promised him, curling her hands around his upper arms.

"I cannae leave her." His brogue thickened as he gasped out the words.

"You must. You're the only one who can reach the doctor in time. I'll have the nurse wake Kenna and we will take care of her." Rowena summoned her inner strength. She could not fail Quinn, not now. This was what she had come here to do, to save him and his child.

"Quinn, get the doctor," she ordered firmly, and before he could protest, she slipped Blair out of his hold and into her own arms. Losing Blair put Quinn into a state of action. He gave himself a little shake and stood.

"Don't let her..." He didn't finish but Rowena knew what he was trying to say. *Don't let her die.*

"She'll be here when you return." Rowena prayed silently that if God was listening, he would answer this one prayer if nothing else. *Let her live. Please.*

Her husband gave a shaky nod and then rushed from the room. Rowena acted instantly. She set Blair back down in her bed and turned to the nurse.

"Wake Kenna at once. Then bring me cold compresses, some ice chips in a bowl, and warm broth."

The old nurse hastily departed. Rowena removed Blair's sweat-drenched nightgown and retrieved a dry cloth and the basin of fresh water from the washstand. She used the cloth to bathe Blair's skin, hoping the cool but not too cold water would bring down her body temperature. By the time the nurse and Kenna returned, Rowena had washed Blair completely, had combed her hair and pulled it back in a knot away from her face and neck, and had changed her into a clean, light nightgown.

"She's a little better, I think," Rowena whispered to Kenna as Quinn's sister took in the sick child with wide, worried eyes.

"Oh, Rowena, if we lose her..." She covered her mouth with the back of her hand.

If they lost Blair, they would lose Quinn.

"We won't," Rowena vowed. She refused to accept that Blair wouldn't get better.

I will do anything I must to keep her safe and well. The fierce protectiveness she felt toward the little girl was overpowering. She may not have given birth to Blair, but Blair was her child now in every way that mattered.

Rowena and Kenna kept a silent vigil at Blair's bedside while they waited for the doctor. When the nurse brought ice chips, they took turns feeding them to Blair by slipping them into her mouth. The girl stirred each time, fussing, but she accepted the little pieces of ice.

"She must continue to take water. The ice chips will help," Rowena explained.

"How do you know all of this?" Kenna asked.

Rowena shrugged. "I had a habit of nursing wounded animals when I was younger. Often, many illnesses are conquered by having the body's temperature lowered and fluids in the body maintained. Water is crucial." She thought of the small fawn she'd nursed back to health a few years before. She and her father had kept it alive in an empty stall in the family stables. She'd fed it a bottle of cow's milk and massaged its weak limbs. After nearly a week, she'd feared the fawn would perish, but it rallied and she and her father were able to turn it loose in the woods.

"She seems to be doing better," Kenna whispered, her eyes fixed on the child's face lit by firelight.

"Yes, I think so," Rowena agreed, and pressed another cool cloth to Blair's forehead.

The door to Blair's room burst open a few moments

later as Quinn and a handsome young man with dark hair came inside. The second man, Dr. McIntosh, held a black medical bag. He immediately set the bag down on the bed next to Rowena and removed his coat, tossing it to the floor, uncaring, as he set about examining his patient.

Everyone held their breath as the doctor carefully looked over Blair, taking her pulse, studying her hands and face, and then listening to her heartbeat.

"She's certainly worse off than yesterday," the doctor murmured. Rowena tensed. "But I see someone has known what to do until I could arrive." McIntosh turned around to look at them. "Who was caring for this child?"

"I was." Rowena stepped forward, her body shaking with worry.

"You did well to bathe her and feed her ice. It has kept her hydrated." The doctor's praise only offered a momentary glow for Rowena before she was back to watching Blair anxiously.

"I will stay and keep watch over her; that's all that can be done for her now. If the fever breaks by morning, she'll be all right," the doctor said.

Kenna placed a hand on the doctor's arm and then escorted the nurse outside, leaving Quinn and Rowena alone with the doctor.

"I'll stay with her," Quinn offered at the same time Rowena settled into a chair near the bed. They looked at each other; then a quiet, deep look passed between them that, for a moment, gave Rowena hope that she hadn't lost her chance at winning Quinn's heart.

"I insist you go to bed. You've done enough for Blair tonight," Quinn said, his voice soft but firm. Yet for some reason his tone made her heart pinch sharply in her chest.

"But I want to stay, please!" She rose from the chair and caught his arm. "She's just as much my child as she is yours." Where her strength to say that came from after all of her exhaustion, she wasn't sure but she had to tell him that, had to make him understand.

"You truly believe that?" Quinn's voice was husky and low, his gray eyes softening to resemble polished moonstones.

"I don't have to believe it. I know it to be true. She is my child, Quinn. I love her." *I love her the way I love you.* "If you stay here with her all night, then so shall I." She met his gaze squarely, unafraid to defy him.

"I think you should let her stay, my lord," the doctor said. "She's taken very good care of the bairn, done as much if not more than I could have when it mattered most. Her fever is already showing signs of breaking."

Quinn's throat worked as he swallowed hard, a single tear escaping his eye as he glanced toward the bed.

"Then sit with me." He took Rowena's hand and led her to the edge of the bed. He leaned back to rest against the wall and pulled Rowena down beside him where they could be close to Blair.

Neither of them spoke, both watching their daughter, worry and hope warring inside them. They didn't touch except to hold hands, and Rowena wished with her all heart she could crawl into his lap and hug him tight. But there was a distance between them, a chasm that hadn't been this vast before.

He isn't ready yet to love me. Admitting this to herself when she'd only carried hope before now seemed to choke her with a silent despair that robbed her of the last of her strength.

Rowena closed her eyes for a moment, just to rest...

When she woke, it was hours later and dawn was coloring the windowpanes of the room with pale pink light. Blair was sleeping on her side, one thumb tucked firmly in her mouth. The doctor was sitting in a chair by the fire, reading a book. He looked up when she stirred. There was no sign of Quinn, and the spot beside her at the foot of Blair's bed was cold when she touched it.

"How is she?" Rowena asked weakly.

"Fine. The fever broke at around half past two this morning. Lord Forres wanted to let you sleep since Blair was doing better."

"Is he...gone?" she asked.

"Yes, once he was assured that Blair was safe and well, he mentioned something about deer stalking and left."

"Left?" The word came out in a higher pitch as she

stared at the doctor in fury. “He left her after she was so ill?”

The doctor closed his book and with a sigh faced Rowena. “He stayed through the worst of it, but I know he was thinking of Lady Forres. I was here when she passed and…well it damned near broke the man. I wouldn’t be angry with him. Give him a few hours to find solace in solitude.”

Rowena’s throat constricted but she managed a nod. Time, he needed time to deal with everything. She’d thought time would be her ally, but now it felt like time had become her foe, keeping her from showing Quinn that he could love again, that he could love *her*.

“Er, Lady Forres, if I may be so bold to ask, would you ever consider working at my clinic in the village? You have a talent for healing and I would love to have a hand from time to time dealing with patients. Nothing risky, of course. I’d keep you well away from the dangerous cases, but for simple injuries and maladies, I could use someone like you as a nurse.”

“A nurse?” She’d never given thought to doing anything aside from running a house and having children, but she had to admit the idea held great appeal.

“Yes, I assume you’ll have your duties here but if you ever decide you wish to do something else, too, I’d be damned glad to have you.”

“What about Kenna?” she asked.

The doctor's handsome face colored. "Er...well, I would but she's not much for the art of healing. She's better at bookkeeping and the like. I could never ask her to work for me, not in that capacity...It wouldn't be proper, not with her being unwed."

"Right," Rowena murmured. "Well, I should like to think on it, being a nurse I mean." She would think on it, but her heart was lifted somewhat at the idea.

At least I could be of use to someone, someone who wanted me around.

"Thank you for staying the night, Dr. McIntosh. Let me have some breakfast brought up." Rowena rose and hastily left the room, not wanting him to see her cry. She'd given up everything to come here with Quinn, but she'd be damned if she let anyone see tears.

Quinn rode out before dawn with Douglas, his gamekeeper. They carried rifles and sat on the backs of garrons, workhorses trained to bring back deer carcasses. The snow had fallen thick the night before and the world was in that quiet state between night and the coming day. The memories from the previous evening hung about Quinn like a heavy shroud.

His mind was cluttered with thoughts, too many to sort through. Blair sick, Rowena taking care of her. Quinn would never have enough words to thank her for saving his daughter's life. Nor could he tell her how hard trusting her had been. He'd had to leave his bairn to fetch McIntosh and there had been a chance he would never see her alive again. But when Rowena had promised him she would keep Blair alive, he'd trusted her. It was the most terrifying thing he had ever done.

And the lass didn't let me down.

He watched the wintry woods around him, his mind barely on the hunt. Douglas had deer stalked with him for many years and knew better than to speak when Quinn clearly needed quiet to think. There was so much to...face.

Blair was already accepting Rowena as part of her life, even saying the word *mama* when asking Rowena to sing to her. She hadn't called Rowena mama yet, but he sensed she was close. Watching them, a woman singing to a babe, a sweet and soft, haunting song. She was so like Maura in that, yet she was different too. She wasn't a replacement; she was nothing like his first wife in looks or temperament, but she needed love as much as any woman and deserved to be loved greatly.

And I'm too bloody scared to let her get close. Because I'm afraid I'll lose my memories of Maura.

With every day that passed, her face faded a little, like an old painting left in a sunny corner of a rarely used room. Blair would have no memories of her mother, and his own were softening too quickly. He was also afraid that if he opened himself up to love again and lost that love, he would never recover. Men didn't survive with shattered hearts, did they? If he hadn't had Blair to comfort him when his first wife had died, he doubted he would have ever been the same. But Blair's sunny face and bright smile, her little chattering voice, and her love of the world had kept hope burning inside him.

Yet he feared that hope, feared what it would cost him if he dared to risk his heart again.

Rowena was too easy to love, too sweet, too sensual, too warm, too...perfect for him. He'd watched her with the servants, his sister, and Blair. His new wife was a natural sweet-tempered creature with the largest heart he'd ever seen.

And I'm the fool who broke it.

"Not too far to the ridge, milord," Douglas said in a low voice.

Quinn answered with a nod. The art of deer stalking was tough and dangerous. No more than one to two hunters at a time could successfully track a red deer into the rocky hills and bring it down.

The morning mists were like milky tendrils through the craggy rocks and the thinning trees when Quinn and Douglas stopped their horses and looped the reins around the low branches of a pine tree.

Quinn collected two rifles for them while Douglas removed the small satchels with their food and flasks of water.

"Dangerous day for this." Douglas pressed his cap on his head and scanned the surrounding lands.

"Aye." Quinn handed Douglas his rifle.

They began the long climb through the mountains. Despite the danger, the surroundings were eerily beautiful. Half-frozen waterfalls cut down through the jagged rocks. Trees stubborn enough to grow out of stone left sparse patches of dark green against the gray mountains before dipping down into the icy lochs. The cold air burned with each breath, clearing the still muddied thoughts in Quinn's head.

The weight of a small dagger in his coat pocket felt like a hundred stones. The dagger that had belonged to his father. The note Rowena had written him was burned into his memory.

Quinn,

I'm sorry for all the pain I've caused you in coming here. I do not regret marrying you, nor do I regret trying to win your heart and loving you as fiercely as I do. But I was foolish to think I could make you love me so soon. I won't trouble you again with confessions of love. I hope someday you might find it in your heart to love me a little. Until then, I shall remain yours,

Rowena.

P.S. This dagger was given to me by a woman who said your father was generous enough to lose it to man in a card game so he could support his family. She wanted you to have it back. Your father sounded like a wonderful man and I wish I could have known him.

Quinn adjusted his rifle and bent low as he crawled along a cluster of rocks. The rough stone would have cut his hands if he hadn't been wearing thick leather gloves. Douglas moved silently beside him.

"Won't be far now. I think I saw some hinds ahead."

Squinting, Quinn peered at the sloping mountain ahead of them. A faint flicker of red amid the gray caught his eye. Eager to climb faster, he placed one foot on a ledge with loose rock. It gave way and he slid, rocks digging into his calves as he regained his footing.

"Careful, milord," Douglas whispered, a steadying hand touching Quinn's back.

"Thank you," he muttered, eyes still fixed on the rocks of the mountain ahead.

The morning mist thinned momentarily and there it was: the nearest hind was prowling up the rocks, head bent as it quested for plants to eat. Quinn waited, studying the deer. It was an older one, a tad feeble. Perfect to target. Removing the weak deer allowed the stronger to breed.

The challenge of deer stalking among the barren, rocky wilderness was that it was hard to cross distances quickly. The herd of hinds and bucks forming a smattering of red spots appeared deceptively close but he knew from years of practice how far away they were. To get to that deer he'd need to find an approach route.

The wind shifted in an instant and a grouse stirred from the rocks ahead, and several of the closest deer sprang up, bolting easily over the tussocks before Quinn could take even one step. The older hind lagged behind, likely too old to catch wind of their scent.

"Come on, I believe we may get it if we move fast." Quinn climbed more quickly, his entire focus on the hunt.

"Watch out—the ledge!" Douglas cried out from behind him as rocks from above tumbled toward them. A buck they hadn't seen north of them had knocked several small boulders loose as he shot higher into the mountain. Quinn ducked as rocks fell past him over the nearby ledge, and one struck his gamekeeper in the chest. Douglas wavered unsteadily inches from the cliff.

"Douglas!" Quinn bellowed, his blood pounding as he lunged for the man.

He caught hold of Douglas's arm a second before the gamekeeper fell over the edge. Crashing to the ground on his stomach, Quinn sucked in painful breaths as he stared over the lip of the cliff. Douglas hung there, cursing and hissing as he clawed at the rocks to find purchase. Quinn's other hand gripped a rock to keep them from sliding off.

"Douglas...," Quinn panted. His shoulder felt like it

was tearing in half. "Can you land below? I could drop you."

"'Tis too far...," Douglas growled. "But you canna lift me back up."

They both knew what Douglas was saying.

Quinn's gritted his teeth and tried to ignore the drop in the pit of his stomach.

"I'll not leave you." He muttered a curse that would have made his mother and father blush.

Inch by agonizing inch, he dragged Douglas up until he saw the man's hands scrabbling at the ledge's edge and then the gamekeeper's grim face appeared as he fought to get up over the cliff.

Quinn only released his hold when the other man was completely safe on the rock shelf; then he fell onto his back, shaking violently. His shoulder jutted out at an unnatural angle and the pain hit him hard enough he tasted bile upon his lips.

"Christ, milord!" Douglas crawled over to him.

Quinn stared up at the gray clouds, blinking slowly as numbing pain overtook him.

"Dislocated shoulder," the gamekeeper muttered, but Quinn could barely hear him. The pain turned from a throbbing sharpness to a slow, burning fire that slowly spread over him.

"Milord, focus. I need to try to move you. I've not set a shoulder back into place before; we need to get you home immediately."

The second he struggled to sit up, the mere movement knocked the breath from his body.

"You've got to stand, milord. We can't stay overnight. I've seen wolves in these woods. Our rifles won't matter if they come prowling."

Douglas was right. They had to move. The thought was sluggish as it floated slowly to the top of his mind.

"Douglas, I can barely breathe," he confessed as the other man tucked his body under Quinn's uninjured arm and helped him stand.

"I know, laddie." The gamekeeper's soft reply was laced with worry. "Keep walking, I'll help ye."

Quinn closed his eyes every time they tried to get past rocky outcrops that required climbing and using his bad shoulder. Each fresh twinge of pain increased that dark haze around the edge of his vision.

"Douglas, you must...distract me. I need to think on something besides the pain."

The gamekeeper huffed as he stepped over a boulder in their descent.

"What about your bride, milord? Surely you want to get home to see her?"

Rowena. The name broke through the darkness like a shaft of sunlight. The dagger and the note still pressed against his heart.

There is a woman who loves me, a woman who wants to heal my broken heart.

Pain surged back into his awareness and he nearly doubled over.

Quinn lifted his head slowly and stared across the vast mountains below them. For an instant he thought he saw...*No, it can't be.* Maura was dead. Yet he'd sworn he saw her figure running down the distant path, her red-gold hair wild and loose in the wind.

"Follow me home." The words were an echo of a distant memory, like the invisible vapors of a fading dream as he woke up, like a thing half remembered yet so familiar.

Quinn's eyes burned and he blinked rapidly.

The sound of Rowena singing, the husky voice of an angel, filled his heart as though Maura's memory had sought him out, showing him the way...the way home.

It flooded the crimson twilight like the close of an Angel's Psalm,

And it lay on my fever'd spirit with a touch of infinite calm.

It quieted pain and sorrow like love overcoming strife...

I have been a fool. A bloody fool.

It was an injustice to Maura's memory to think she would be erased by his love for another woman. She would not have wanted him suffering a broken heart. She would have *wanted* him to be happy, to find a woman who loved him and who loved Blair. And that woman was at his home, brokenhearted for loving him, a man with a stone heart. But his heart wasn't stone anymore. It felt too soft, wounded and bleeding all over again. Yet he embraced the pain for the first time in a year because the pain meant he was alive. The real ghost in his life was never Maura; it was *him*.

I want to live again. I'm tired of the past, tired of the pain.

Rowena was his salvation. He'd thought he wasn't able to love, was too afraid to love, but the truth was…he'd been falling in love with her since the moment she'd rescued Blair at the fountain. He'd simply been too blind to see the truth staring him right in the face.

I must find my way home to Rowena.

Chapter Twelve

Rowena stared at the cold bowl of soup and sighed.

"Kenna, he's still not back…" She glanced at Quinn's sister, who sat across from her at the lonely length of the dining room table.

"I'm sure he's all right. Douglas is with him. They've been deer stalking together since Quinn was seventeen." Despite her reassuring words, Kenna's face was tight with worry.

"Twelve hours…" Rowena had counted the seconds since luncheon had come and gone. Now dinner was well past, but the servants hadn't removed her food, not when she continued to stare at it numbly. She'd spent much of the day with Blair, relieved to see Dr. McIntosh was right and that she was indeed feeling better.

"Why don't you go up to bed," Kenna suggested.

"He'll come home after you've fallen asleep." Kenna stood up and waved an anxious footman to clear away the dishes.

"It's too late. We should go look for them." Rowena glanced at the tall clock in the corner of the dining room. Something twisted in her stomach and dread gripped her heart in its icy claws.

"We could send a few men." Quinn's sister finally agreed.

Rowena was on her feet and waving to a footman. "Please have Mr. Morris meet Kenna and me by the door. I'll need a heavy coat and mittens. Oh, and a scarf."

"Rowena, you can't go out. You're not used to the winters this far north." Kenna gently took her by the arm but Rowena pulled away.

"I have to go." How could she explain it to the other woman? Something in her bones was telling her she had to find Quinn and bring him home. She had to swallow down the fear and anxiety that something terrible might have happened. *He's going to be fine. I will find him and bring him home.*

Kenna followed her out to the main hall where Morris, five footmen, and two grooms were all pulling on coats and gloves.

"My lady, you'd best stay here," Mr. Morris said, his voice gruff, the scowl on his face disapproving.

Staring at him, fury and fear collided inside of her.

This man had no right to order *her* about. She was the Countess of Forres. It was up to her to make decisions.

"Mr. Morris, you will remember to whom you are speaking. My husband is out there somewhere and he needs me. I *am* going."

A commotion at the top of the stairs prevented them from arguing further. The nurse was carrying a crying Blair in her arms. The little girl's eyes were red and puffy and her cheeks were splotched with color.

"Blair, what's the matter?" Rowena and Kenna met the nurse at the bottom of the stairs.

"She's had a wee bad dream. She wants to see her papa. Where is the master?" The old nurse glanced around and then frowned at the sight of the men grouped in the entryway, all dressed in their outer gear.

"Where's Papa?" Blair sniffed and a fat tear rolled down the tip of her little nose.

"Papa is out hunting." Rowena took Blair from the nurse and cradled her against her chest.

"Bad dreams...," Blair whispered. "Have bad ones. Do you get them?" she asked with such a desperate yet sweet earnestness that it broke Rowena's heart.

"I do sometimes. But they are only dreams. You will be safe now that you're awake. But don't be frightened. Aunt Kenna is here. She'll sing you to sleep."

The babe's eyes widened. "You're leaving, Mama?"

The hall grew deathly silent as the word Blair had uttered sank in.

Mama.

Rowena's heart grew even more inside her chest, strengthened by that single word. *I am her mother and I will bring her father home safe.* With every servant watching her with sharp gazes, Rowena kissed Blair's forehead. The soft scent of Blair's skin made her want to stay there and cradle the child to her, but she had to leave. Quinn needed her.

"I must go for a short while, sweetheart. Someone must bring your papa home." The words came out of her throat raw. She didn't want to leave Blair behind, not after being called Mama, but she had to find Quinn.

"Take care of her, Kenna." Rowena hugged Blair and handed her over; then she grabbed her coat from a footman and pulled it on.

Morris opened his mouth but she cut him off.

"You've no right to tell me I cannot go out and rescue the man I love. If you try, I'll send you packing." She shot him a steely gaze and the older butler nodded in grudging respect.

"Very well, my lady, but I will insist on going with you."

The grooms had ponies ready and Rowena mounted hers quickly. The search party headed north to the low-lying hills, searching for any signs of Quinn as darkness consumed the light inch by inch. The ponies plunged through the heavy snow, trekking farther and farther north.

"We're nearly to the mountains." Morris approached her side, a red scarf covering his face and muffling his voice a little.

Rowena squinted at the thinning trees and the steep, rocky path half a mile ahead.

"We have to leave the horses and walk the rest of the way," Morris added, and to Rowena's surprise, he aided her in dismounting.

The clouds overhead began to unleash a wave of fresh snow and the search party had to fight and claw their way to the base of the hills. The wind was bitter and piercing, knifing through her gloves to slash at her hands and suck away any bit of heat her body still possessed.

Quinn, where are you? She squinted through the darkness and the heavy snow, but had to close her eyes. She stopped moving, her body shaking violently as the cold moved through her body. A woman's face suddenly flashed in her mind. Eyes bright and her lips parted as she drew in a quick breath; then her face was gone, but a faint whisper barely audible above the winds teased Rowena's ears.

"Follow me."

Rowena jolted awake from the strange trance and glanced around. She could not see any of the others from the search party. She was alone. Oh God, she was going to freeze to death out here...

A veil of snow parted ahead and a feminine figure appeared. A woman in a cloak, with a solemn gaze. Staring in shock, Rowena couldn't move or speak. There couldn't be a woman out here in the snow; she was the only female who'd gone out with the search party.

"Rowena..." The woman's voice drew her name out soft and sorrowful like a plaintive call of a nightingale. *"Follow me."*

Rowena moved, step by painful step, toward the figure ahead. She wasn't sure how long she trudged through the snow. Minutes, hours, it all blurred together.

"Wait...," she croaked as the figure began to fade into the night.

"Help!" A throaty voice broke through the gloom as the snowfall lessened.

"Here!" Rowena cried as she spied a huddled mass twenty feet ahead at the base of a tree. When she reached the tree, she collapsed to her knees and came face-to-face with Douglas the gamekeeper. He had his arms wrapped around Quinn's limp form.

"What happened?" Rowena asked as she started to lift Quinn by one arm but Douglas shouted.

"No! He's got a dislocated shoulder. Lift him by the waist." Douglas threw Quinn's good arm over his shoulder and Rowena gripped her husband's waist.

"Come on, laddie. Wake up," Douglas growled, and jostled Quinn roughly.

"Douglas?" Quinn's voice was low and drowsy as his head lifted. "Are we home yet?"

Rowena gripped him tighter, hugging him close. "I'm here," she told him.

His dazed gaze fell upon her and he smiled through obvious pain.

"My bold, brave lass." He tried to kiss her but he didn't have enough mobility.

"Hold that thought, laddie," Douglas snapped. "You can woo your wife when we're safely home."

The three of them hobbled through the snow but their passage was easier as the snowfall stopped and the clouds parted, revealing a nearly full moon. The only shadows around were rocks and trees as they walked back down the hills. Rowena tried not to think about how isolated they were. *Will we ever find our way home?*

The wind carried an eerie whine that soon turned into a recognizable shout.

"My lady?" Morris's voice boomed out in the distance. "Where are you?"

"Morris!" Douglas bellowed. "She's here!"

Distant shadows moved closer until the search party was surrounding them. Rowena came face-to-face with the butler, and when he saw her holding up Quinn, a flash of shock and relief, then deep, honest respect glowed in his gaze.

"You found him," Morris exhaled. "We lost you in the storm but found their garrons by a copse of trees. We got turned around and we would not have found Douglas or his lordship, but you did..."

The thought went unfinished but Rowena understood. If she hadn't found Quinn and Douglas, no one would have and they may not have survived the night.

Morris took Rowena's place, holding Quinn's waist as they walked back to the ponies. It took a lot of work but Rowena helped Quinn onto a horse behind Morris and they were able to strap him to the butler using a belt from one of the grooms.

It took two hours to reach the house and Kenna was the first to rush out to meet them. She caught sight of Quinn's ashen face and had a groom ride to the village for the doctor.

Quinn was taken upstairs to his chamber and stripped out of his soaked hunting clothes and put to bed with a roaring fire close by. Morris and Mrs. Stuart marshaled the servants into their chores while everyone waited for the doctor to arrive.

Rowena stood by the bed, leaning against one post and watching Quinn sleep.

"My lady," Douglas whispered as he joined her. "It's

my fault we had an accident whilst hunting. I lost my footing and fell. His lordship saved me."

She heard the catch in the gamekeeper's tone but she could not look away from Quinn's face to see him.

"Douglas, can you see if Blair is still awake? If she is, bring her here. If she's sleeping, let her sleep."

"Of course, my lady." Douglas bowed and exited the chamber.

Rowena left the bedpost and walked over to sit on the edge of the bed closest to Quinn. Dark hair fell across his forehead and she brushed it back.

"I found you," she whispered. The long dark lashes on his cheek, which she'd been counting as he slept, fluttered and his pain-filled gaze settled on her.

"Rowena." Her name came out soft, each syllable uttered gently as though he took care in speaking her name. He lifted one hand.

"You need to sleep." She placed her fingers in his and he gripped them with surprising strength.

"I've been a fool." He uttered the words harshly, his eyes darkening as he struggled to continue. "I believed I was not ready, not in my heart. But from the moment I saw you save my child, I knew I would love you. How could I not? Beautiful, intelligent, and compassionate? I did not think fate would be so kind as to give you to me, but here you are." A smile curved his lips. "I only wonder if I'll ever be able to earn your forgiveness."

Tears coated Rowena's eyelashes as she pressed his hand to her cheek and fought off the urge to cry.

"There's nothing to forgive. You love her still and I understand. Not all hearts can be mended. All I ask is that you let me love you, let me be with you."

Quinn shook his head. "No, you don't understand—"

The bedchamber door opened and Dr. McIntosh entered, followed by Kenna. He stroked his mustache and shook his head.

"My lord, I heard you've put your shoulder out. Three visits in as many days, perhaps I ought to move my clinic to the castle." The doctor set his black leather medical bag at the foot of the bed and nodded to Rowena in greeting. "My lady."

"I'm afraid we seem to be quite helpless without you, Dr. McIntosh." Quinn's wry chuckle turned into a moan as the doctor helped him to sit up. Rowena watched in fascination as the doctor lifted Quinn's injured arm and with a series of slow gentle motions, he worked the shoulder back into place. Rowena held Quinn's other hand and kept her eyes locked with his.

"Ahh..." Quinn hissed, then his features softened and he released a slow breath.

"Better?" McIntosh asked.

"Much," Quinn replied, a little breathless, but the pain in his expression was quickly fading.

"Good." The doctor used a strip of white cloth to

make a sling and gave Quinn a tiny bit of morphine for the pain that would help him sleep.

"Thank you, Ian," Kenna murmured, blushing as she took the doctor's arm. "'Tis late. Why don't I get some tea and biscuits and have a room readied for you?"

The doctor smiled sheepishly at Kenna. "Er...yes, that would be wonderful." He leaned a little closer to Kenna, smiling.

Rowena watched them go and Douglas reappeared. "The wee bairn is asleep."

"Thank you, Douglas. I'll tell her about her papa in the morning." Rowena closed the door behind him and sagged against the wood.

"Is Blair all right? When I left this morning, McIntosh said she was fine. I wouldn't have left if she'd been..." Quinn's face was strained with fear and pain.

"She is fine," Rowena assured him. "She merely had a bad dream and was wishing you were here."

"I'm sorry I left," he whispered. "I shouldnae have left you, either of you." His brogue thickened as the morphine he'd been given began to take hold. Soon he would be resting and she could warm up. His eyelids closed and he exhaled deeply as he sank into sleep.

She was still in her soaked clothes and the tingling in her limbs was settling in. She glanced at Quinn, now sleeping on the bed. Surely he would not mind if she used his bath in the adjoining room. She tugged on the bell cord and Gwen appeared.

"Mr. Morris thought you might need me, my lady. I was preparing a bowl of hot beef stew and some fresh bread."

"That would be wonderful. But first, could you draw me a bath and help me undress?"

"Of course." The maid helped her strip out of her wet clothes after a hot bath was ready.

Rowena sank into the deep tub of hot water, relieved at the way her bones stopped trembling with such force that her teeth had been rattling in her skull. The night's memories came rushing back to her. How she'd struggled through the cold and dark, her heart starting to die with Quinn. Wanting to save him even when she knew he'd never love her...Then she'd heard it. That ethereal voice through the veil of snow. And she'd seen that figure beckoning to her.

A ghost? A phantom leading her to Quinn so she might save him? Her skin was covered with goose bumps and she rubbed her arms. Whatever it had been, it had helped her find him and bring him home.

She sank below the water, running her hands through the silken strands of her hair before coming back up for air.

"Wife, I have more I need to say." Quinn's rough, low voice echoed through the bathroom and startled Rowena.

He was leaning in the doorway, resting against his good shoulder, his lips curved in gentle amusement. Her heart leapt inside her.

"I thought you were asleep. The morphine..."

Quinn barked out a laugh. "You've got a lot to learn about a Scotsman. A wee bit of that won't keep me down for long." He adjusted the sling on his arm and walked over to her, a lazy grin spreading on his face.

"What are you doing? You should stay in bed and rest." She sank deeper into the tub, a little shy after what had last happened between them and how exposed she still felt after having given him her heart and not being loved back. She needed time to adjust to living with him and not being loved by him. Being close to him like this would not help her heal her broken heart.

Her husband shook his head and with his good arm crooked a finger.

"It's time we talked, Rowena. There are things that need to be said and I would like to do that in my bed with naught but our skin between us."

Chapter Thirteen

With nothing but skin between them?

Rowena's mouth dropped open. "But—"

"No buts. Out of the tub, Wife." He reached for a bath towel and held it out to her. She knew by the gleam in his eyes that he wouldn't turn his back on her when she was getting out. The thought of standing in front of him, entirely naked, excited her and yet she was nervous too. Swallowing, she got out of the tub, water cascading down her body, and she reached for the towel. For a brief instant, Quinn tugged the towel out of her reach before he let her fingers grasp it.

Chuckling, he waited for her to dry herself off and then he dropped the towel to the floor again.

"My bed, now," he ordered, and the slight edge to his

tone sent a flutter of excitement through Rowena that shocked her.

She padded over to the big bed and climbed beneath the blankets, pulling them high up to her chin. Quinn rolled his eyes.

"One of these days, you'll learn not to be so modest, Wife." He eased down onto the bed beside her. His good side was closest to her and he lifted his arm to curl it around her waist and pull her against him.

"Quinn, we shouldn't do anything, your arm."

"Hush, lass, we won't. I just want your full attention. Having you bare keeps your mind on me."

She almost laughed. How could she not think of him? Rowena stared at him, a little shocked and amused and definitely scandalized. "Very well, you have my attention." She cuddled closer, her bare legs sliding over his trouser-clad ones beneath the blankets.

"What you said before, about my first wife." In the time it took him to pause, Rowena's stomach clenched in dread. A moment ago, she'd been comfortable enough to relax, and now there was no way she could handle this. He was going to tell her he couldn't love her again.

"Please, don't tell me. I don't need to hear it." She tried to escape his arms, but he kept her firmly in his hold.

He covered her lips with his, silencing any further protests.

It was a sweet kiss, but his lips took their time

exploring hers, and when they finally broke apart, he was smiling at her. The affection in his expression stole her breath.

"You *need* to hear this. And I need to say it. I'm not a man for speaking from my heart, but there are things I must tell you now."

She glanced away, unable to face him in case he broke her heart again.

"I will always love my first wife. But that doesn't mean I can never love another woman again. I thought that I couldn't. But I was wrong." He was silent for a long moment and Rowena held her breath.

"You have me, Rowena. That's what I'm trying to say." He stared at her, all seriousness as he met her gaze.

It wasn't *I love you* but it was something close enough that the hope she'd buried resurfaced. Love might come after all. His eyes were full of light and affection; none of the guilt and regret she'd grown accustomed to was there. It had vanished. She was afraid to wish what he was saying was true, and yet her love for him began to burn through her, like a star in a winter sky, brightly shining through in piercing clarity.

"Do you forgive me? I was a bloody fool, trying to stay away from you. You needed me, needed my love and I failed you." He glanced down at his arm in the sling. "If it wasn't for this arm, I'd be showing you how sorry I am."

Rowena pressed her cheek to his shoulder and rubbed

her face against his shirt. His scent was masculine and clean with a hint of the woods.

"We can talk in the morning," she murmured, and pulled the blankets higher.

"Agreed, but first you'll eat. They brought up supper while you were bathing." He nodded at the tray of food in the corner of the room. He left the bed to bring it to her. Rowena ate, a little shy at Quinn's fixed fascination. There was a reverence in his expression toward her that made her blush and it was mixed with puzzlement.

"How did you find me in the storm?"

Swallowing, she peered up at him. There was no way she would tell him the truth. That a woman, or some type of vision, perhaps a dream, led her to him.

"I got turned around somehow. I heard someone calling me to follow and I found you. I cannot really explain it."

Quinn didn't say anything to that but when she finished eating, he carried the tray away from the bed, turned down the oil lamps, and then climbed back into bed with her.

"Come here, wee one," he teased softly, and tickled her bare waist. It was scandalous to be completely naked in bed while he was still halfway dressed, but Rowena reveled in the decadence of the soft sheets against her skin and the muscled lines of Quinn's body beside her.

"Christmas is only a week away. What do you want as a present, Wife?"

Rowena kissed his cheek, fighting back a quivering emotion in her chest. "Just you."

Quinn chuckled. "Very well, I'll have to guess, then, won't I?"

A little smile curved Rowena's lips. "Perhaps." At that moment she had no need or desire for anything else. Quinn was all she wanted.

Quinn watched his wife and daughter standing in front of the tall Christmas tree in the grand hall. Two footmen on ladders were stringing silver strands of tinsel around the branches.

"Mama!" Blair scampered about on her little chubby legs, her hair adorned with a fat red satin ribbon that made the gold strands shine like a halo from an angel.

"Sweetheart." Rowena caught the little girl under her arms and spun her around. The sight filled Quinn with joy. A joy he'd never thought he could feel again after losing Maura. Hearing Blair call Rowena *Mama* no longer hurt. Not since that night on the mountain when he'd seen Maura through the snow leading him home to his wife.

Everything was all right now. Rowena was settling into his home at last. And the servants had turned into loyal supporters of her since she'd rescued him. Quinn had even overhead Morris say she was a lady of miracles. The changes in the house were fast and wonderful. Laughter, life, love...it was all there, everything he'd missed since Maura died.

"Quinn! Come help!" Rowena called out, and lifted a box of ornaments up for him to see. Her ruby-red dress was a lush creation of ruffles and small bustles in the back. The bodice was embroidered with silver swans and golden stars. Her blond hair was pulled up in another elegant coiffure. A picture of grace, beauty, and the spirit of Christmas. And she was all his.

I'm twice blessed.

Quinn was determined to make this Christmas holiday wonderful for his new wife, and he knew, after five days of careful planning and thought, just what that would be. The gift was due to arrive at any minute.

When one of the footmen struggled to reach for the top of the tree with a star ornament, Quinn rushed forward.

"Let me." He held the ladder steady so the young man could climb back down and Quinn took charge of the star and took the lad's place on the ladder, careful not to twinge his arm, which was still in a sling. As he settled the star in place, the servants applauded.

"Oh bravo, Quinn." Rowena joined him at the bottom of the ladder, her blue eyes bright. "It's nearly time for Christmas dinner." She reached down to grab Blair's hand as the child wandered over to them.

"Pick me up, Papa!" Blair waved her free hand in the air.

"Oh, all right, you wee scamp." He laughed and picked her up and settled her on his hip opposite his bad arm. He bounced her there, earning him delighted squeals.

Morris appeared in the doorway, a little smile hovering about his usually serious mouth.

"My lord, we have...visitors."

"Visitors? In this weather?" Rowena's brow furrowed and she took Blair from his arms and passed her to the nurse.

"Yes, my lady." Morris nodded. "I escorted them to the drawing room."

"Thank you, Morris." Quinn had to fight off a grin as he escorted Rowena toward the drawing room.

"Who do you suppose..." she began as they reached the drawing room. The rumble of voices silenced her.

The firelight from the room lit up her face the instant

she realized who the voices belonged to. Her eyes widened and her lips parted; then she turned her face to his and the love shining in her eyes burned him clear through.

"Did you..." She couldn't seem to finish the thought and she didn't need to.

"I may have sent a telegram or two and arranged for transportation."

"I *love* you." The little whisper curled around his heart, twining itself deep enough that it could never be removed.

"I know." He brushed the backs of his knuckles over her cheek and then gave her an encouraging nod.

Rowena bit her lip and then rushed into the drawing room.

"Rowena!" the voices all chimed in as she was spotted.

Quinn leaned one shoulder against the open doorway and watched the scene. Rowena was hugging her parents, while Milly and her husband stood a few feet away, both smiling. Hadley had his arms around Rowena's sister and looked every inch a man satisfied with life.

"Forres, there you are." Lord Pepperwirth waved a hand at him. "Come in and tell us how our grandchild is."

It never ceased to amaze him how deep the love the Pepperwirths had for strangers. Blair was not of their blood, but they treated her as though she was.

I made the right choice. For my household, my daughter,

and me. Tonight, after dinner, he would show Rowena how much he cared about her.

The snow began to fall just after midnight, and Rowena took her fur stole and walked out onto the snow-covered terrace. Inside the house, the servants were rushing to put out the lights and head to bed. The whispers, the muted laughter, the joys of the holiday surrounded her like a warm embrace from an invisible force of love.

"There you are." Quinn's deep voice did not startle her. She was lost in her daydreams that danced among the falling snowflakes. The crunch of his boots behind her and the pressure of his hands on her shoulders seemed almost surreal.

"Did you like my present?"

She turned in his arms at the teasing question. When she pretended to think on her answer, he dragged her against him and slanted his mouth over hers. His arms encompassed more than her body. It was as though he held her soul in his hands in that moment. Every pain, every hurt suffered in trying to win his heart was fading in the fire of the passion and the love that filled her to bursting.

"Take me to bed, Husband," she murmured against his lips.

"Of course." His lips curved in a smile and she gasped as he bent and scooped her up in his arms, skirts and all, in his arms to carry her back inside.

At the foot of the stairs, they passed a flustered Mrs. Stuart, who blushed when she saw them.

"Enjoy your night, Mrs. Stuart," Quinn called over his shoulder as he carried Rowena up the stairs and to his bedchamber. The door was open and Quinn's valet was pulling back the sheets on the bed.

"Pardon me." The young man fled from the room.

Quinn laid Rowena on the bed and rolled her over onto her stomach. She sucked in a breath as she saw Quinn in the mirror withdraw his father's slim dagger. He lowered the blade to her back. A rush of snapping sounds and then the dress and corset sagged loose beneath her. She met Quinn's gaze in the mirror and he shrugged one shoulder.

"I did not want to bother with the laces."

She moved to sit up on the bed, but the dress slid down to her hips. Quinn gestured with the knife like a roguish pirate. "Strip, lassie."

Smiling, she stood and let the red satin fall into a puddle at her feet. Then she unlaced the front of her chemise and let it drop off her shoulders to the ground.

Quinn set the blade on the table beside the bed and removed his coat and waistcoat, and pulled his shirt over his head. The sight of his bare chest never failed to excite her. She lifted her hands to his chest, stroking over his hot skin, marveling at how the muscles were taut and firm.

"You did not answer my question. Did you like the present I gave you?" His gray eyes sparked with heat as he curved his palms over her bottom and squeezed gently. Heat flamed between her thighs and a shiver of desire moved through her.

"I'll tell you...after." She tiptoed her fingers down to his trousers, where she unfastened them and tugged them down. He kicked the pants away and lifted her up his body to set her on the bed. Then he leaned over her, kissing her deeply, their tongues playing as he got her to move back on the bed.

Rowena lay down as Quinn crawled over her and nudged her thighs apart. She always felt so vulnerable when he covered her like this. She was open to him, to let him do anything to her. He stroked her folds with one hand, teasing her body until she was wet and aching for him. Then he entered her with one rapid thrust that had them both groaning in pleasure. Their gazes locked as he captured her hands in his, lacing their fingers together on either side of her head. They rocked together, their bodies merging into one.

"Rowena, I've not said it," he whispered huskily.

She struggled to focus on his words. "Said…what?"

He kissed her lips, nibbled at her neck, and bit down lightly on her shoulder until she arched her hips, and his body spasmed in building pleasure. He didn't speak again. He was lost in the blinding, exquisite experience of making love; she saw it in his face as he watched her, a feral desire burning in the silver depths of his eyes.

"Ahh!" She exploded into wave after wave of pleasure. He came seconds later, shouting her name in a rough cry.

They seemed to float down from the clouds together. Rowena cradled her to him as he regained his breath. His stare was searching as he looked down at her.

"What I am trying to say is that I *love* you." He didn't look away, didn't blink.

"What?" Her eyes began to sting. *Had she really heard that?*

"I did not understand, not until now, tonight, that love isn't always a lightning strike. Sometimes…" He paused to tuck a lock of hair behind her ear. "Sometimes it comes slowly, like a building sunrise. The waves of color, full of life, began to pierce the darkness, made it fade, minute by minute, hour by hour." His lashes lowered to half-mast as he stared at her mouth and caressed her lips with the pad of his thumb.

Rowena held her breath. His words were tearing her

apart, then building her back together, making her stronger somehow.

"I knew I loved you that day upon the hill during the storm," she admitted. "There was never going to be anyone else for me. Not after that. You were in my dreams."

Her confession earned a smile from his too-serious face.

"I love you, Rowena. I love you as much as I can love anyone. You are in my heart. You own me heart, body, and soul," he vowed, and raised one of her hands to his chest. The look in his eyes was earnest and steadfast. A vow that went both ways. A vow that would not be broken. "I could not believe that love was possible again. Not after losing Maura, but then you came into my life. A ray of endless light, an ever-coming dawn." He lowered his head and kissed her. Slow, deep, filling her heart with everything he could give. She wrapped her arms around his neck, holding him close as she kissed him back. Outside their bedroom window, the snow continued to fall and the northern winds upon the distant mountains carried a soft half-forgotten song of a woman long gone as her spirit was at last put to rest.

"I finally have my Christmas wish, the present I truly wanted."

He raised a brow and half smiled. "And what is it?"

"To win a Scottish lord's heart."

Thank you for reading *A Scottish Lord for Christmas*! Have you read the first book in the series *An Earl by Any Other Name*? Turn the page to read the first three chapters.

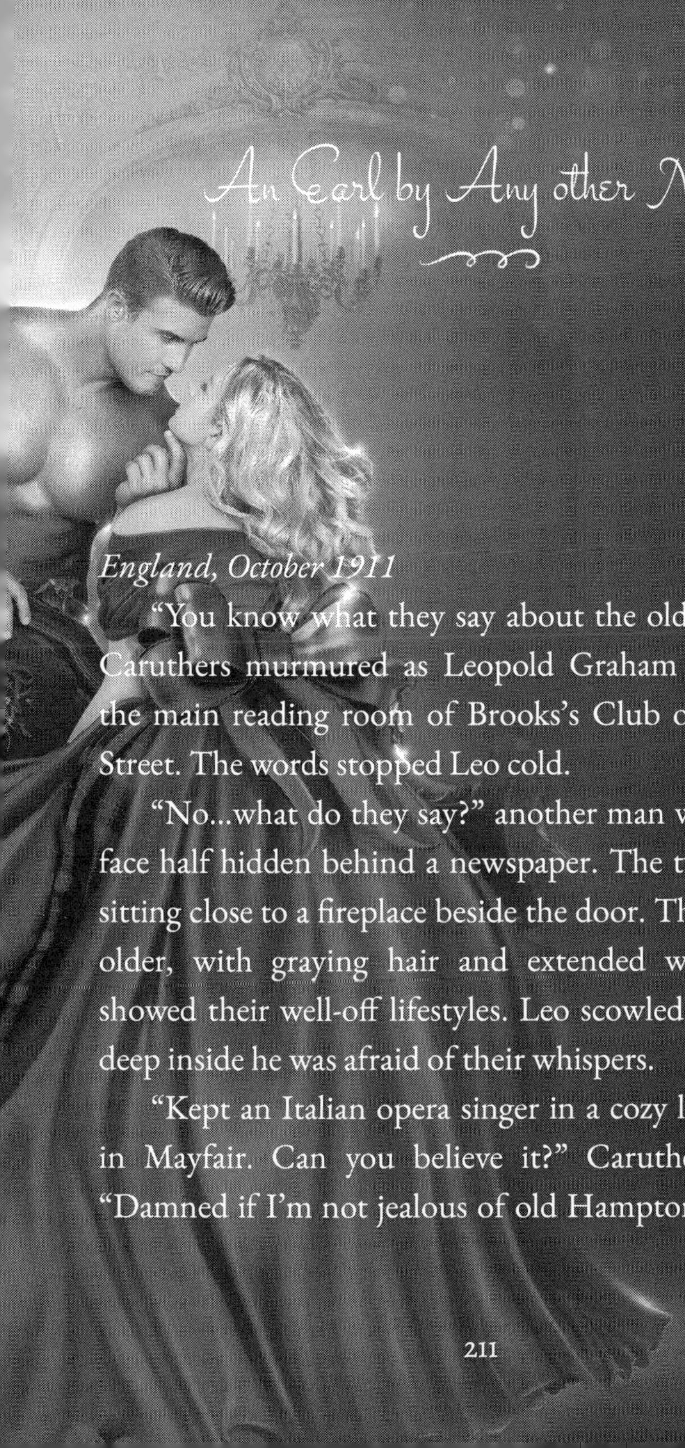

An Earl by Any other Name

England, October 1911

"You know what they say about the old boy..." Lord Caruthers murmured as Leopold Graham stepped into the main reading room of Brooks's Club on St. James's Street. The words stopped Leo cold.

"No...what do they say?" another man whispered, his face half hidden behind a newspaper. The two men were sitting close to a fireplace beside the door. They were both older, with graying hair and extended waistlines that showed their well-off lifestyles. Leo scowled at them, but deep inside he was afraid of their whispers.

"Kept an Italian opera singer in a cozy little love nest in Mayfair. Can you believe it?" Caruthers chuckled. "Damned if I'm not jealous of old Hampton for carrying on like that with a wife and son at home. Quite a bold move to bring down scandal like that so publically."

"Wait..." The other man gasped, his paper rattling in his hands with excitement as he leaned closer to Caruthers. "The old fellow who died in his mistress's bed? I heard about that!" The older gentlemen were leaning close to each other, gossiping like a pair of old ladies, using their newspapers much the way women would use fans.

"Yes! The late Lord Hampton...Had to carry him out of that woman's house. She didn't even care about him. I heard she was determined to keep the home. Messy business leaving that to the son to deal with. Even now that the family is out of their year of mourning, everyone hasn't forgotten old Hampton's sins." Caruthers sniffed pompously. "I wouldn't let my son be seen at dinner with that family, not with that sort of talk still hanging about."

"Indeed," the other man agreed. "Quite so—"

"Ahem," Leo growled softly as he stalked past the two men, his fists clenched in rage. Both of them jumped; apparently they'd deceived themselves into thinking he couldn't hear them. *Deaf old fools*. Even at his own bloody club, he couldn't escape the rumors, the whispering, the damned utter black scandal that his late father had brought down on his head. He didn't want to remember having to deal with his father's mistress or paying her off by letting her keep the house his father had purchased.

The need to silence her and quiet the scandal as quickly as he could hadn't been as successful as he'd hoped. London ballrooms and dinners caught rumors and scandals, spreading them like wildfire.

Caruthers and his companion, now silent, watched him with keen interest as he settled in the only empty seat, one by the window facing St. James Street. On the street there was a mixture of motorcars and carriages. London was always busy in the fall with the season in full swing. For a brief moment, he let his thoughts wander away from the pain of listening to his family's private business be fodder for entertainment. If only he could get in his car and drive away from it all...

Despite the silence in the room, Leo knew that every man was focused on him.

He raked a hand through his blond hair and stifled a groan. He'd been in London for all of three days, feverishly trying to secure investment opportunities and join in speculation schemes but it was no use. No one would work with him.

Father has damned me and Mother for his selfishness!

The spike of rage inside Leo was startling and so unlike him, but after having more than one door closed in his face today, he was exhausted. Even though it had been a year since his father had died, the scandal and the fervor behind it had yet to fade. His poor mother, Mina, refused to leave the countryside, knowing she'd have no real friends left in London who would allow her entrance to their homes. All because his father hadn't been faithful. It was an accepted albeit awful practice for a man to carry on an affair, but a man didn't die in his mistress's bed after a night of bed play, and he certainly didn't wrack up debts to pay for the care and keeping of that mistress. Yet that was exactly what his father had done.

Leo reached into his pocket and removed a letter that his footman had delivered to him before he'd left for the club. He opened it, smoothing out the paper and reading the hastily written lines from his banker, praying for much needed good news.

Lord Hampton,

It is with my deepest regret that we cannot extend any of your family's lines of credit at this time. We will be happy to discuss more credit if you can bring us new collateral but until then, the estate and all of your tenant farms connected thereto are fully mortgaged and cannot be further used to obtain additional credit.

Sincerely,

Thomas Atkinson

The words filled Leo's stomach with an empty ache. He had to find a way to stabilize his family's estate or he would risk losing his mansion in the country. Hampton

House was his home, more so than London ever would be, and to think of creditors pawing at his family's furniture and running amok through the rooms of his childhood...

I won't let it happen. He would find someone to invest with, and he would bury his father's scandal in whatever way he could by living a life above society's reproach. He was going to marry a good English rose and not make the same mistakes his father did by allowing himself to become obsessed with some exotic beauty. Those sort of women were *always* trouble.

He had always believed he might marry someday for love and have a wife who was as passionate as he was, but those dreams were dashed now. He had chosen a neighboring viscount's daughter as his future bride for financial reasons. It was a chilling thought that he would soon tie his future to a woman without love, but it must be done.

"Hampton?" A familiar voice shook him from his dark thoughts. Striding toward him was a man he recognized.

"Hadley!" He grinned as relief at his friend's appearance swept through him. He got to his feet and shook Owen Hadley's hand. His dark-haired friend was smiling widely. Once, as boys at Eton, they had been inseparable, but then Owen and their friend Jack had gone off to fight in South Africa in the Second Boer War. When they returned, Jack and Owen had...changed. Leo hadn't been able to leave to go fight; his father hadn't allowed it. The estate was entailed to a male heir and as the only son, if Leo had perished beneath an African sun, some distant cousin would have taken over Hampton.

"Haven't seen you at the club in ages." Hadley sat across from him at the small table beside the window. It didn't escape Leo's notice that Hadley's clothes, while finely tailored, were a season out of fashion. Money troubles were apparently all the rage this season for young bachelors. Leo had enough money to pay his creditors now, but if he didn't find a way to produce new income soon, he would be in trouble.

"I've been in the country." Leo hastily tucked the banker's letter back into his coat pocket.

Owen's keen eyes missed little but he didn't ask what the letter was about. "You look tired, old friend."

"Do I?" Leo mused glumly. "Since my father died, it has been a trial to set the estate to rights."

"Are you afraid you'll lose it?" Owen asked quietly.

"No...at least not yet." Leo sighed. "But I cannot get a single man in London to let me partake in investments or speculation. The economy of the tenant farms simply isn't what it used to be and we need more stability." He leaned back in the leather armchair, wishing he could stay here in the club and not have to face the world outside.

"Cheer up!" Owen grinned. "Why don't we go find

something to entertain us? It's been months and you could use some fun."

Leo shook his head. As much as he wished to throw his cares to the wind, he couldn't. His father's scandal had forced him to live a life of boredom. It was the only way he might find favor with society again, and that was crucial if he was to preserve Hampton House and everyone who depended on him.

"Perhaps another time. I suppose I ought to get back to Hampton at any rate. Lord knows what Mother will have gotten up to while I was away."

His friend laughed heartily. "Your mother is a dear. Any trouble she causes is a delight."

Leo brushed his hair back from his eyes. "You don't have to live with her."

"Touché." Owen shrugged. "At least she's not involved with those suffragettes. You know they're having meetings all over the country right now?"

"Lord, don't even breathe a word of women's rights around my mother." Leo and Owen both glanced around the club to make sure no one was listening. Talking of suffragettes had a way of rousing trouble in a gentleman's club, one of the few places that completely barred women.

"Well, I won't keep you, Hampton, but write to me the next time you're in town. We should have a drink."

"Agreed." Leo shook Owen's hand and they both rose from their chairs. It would have been a fine thing to sit and talk with his old friend. They'd survived much together, but after today with his failures and knowing the talk of scandal was still clinging to his family even after a year, he was ready to run home with his tail tucked firmly between his legs. Tomorrow he would find another way to protect his home...tomorrow.

Chapter 2

"Now that your father is dead, I intend to indulge in scandalous behavior."

Leo choked on the sandwich he'd just bitten into. He'd been back from London for only one day, and his mother was already trying to kill him. His gaze shot to her face. The Dowager Countess of Hampton slid into a chair opposite him at the large oak dining room table where he was currently eating luncheon. She smoothed her lace tea gown over her lap and fixed him with a steady gaze.

Blood roared through his ears as he struggled to dislodge the bit of sandwich from his throat. *Damn cucumber...can't get it out...* He coughed violently and was finally able to get a bit of breath back in his lungs.

"Breathe, my dear, breathe," she intoned gently as though instructing a child of four, not her grown son of thirty-two. He adored his mother, but she had the uncanny ability of rankling him when he least needed to be rankled.

He reached forward and snatched his water goblet, hastily gulping the liquid. A cold nose nudged his other hand and he glanced down, seeing Ladybird, his chocolate-colored English cocker spaniel, lean against his knee. She whined softly when their eyes met. At least there was one sympathetic female in this house that wasn't determined to do him in.

"Mother," Leo finally got out. "What on earth are you talking about?" Could a man not enjoy a simple meal in peace? His eyes flicked heavenward as he prayed for patience. He supposed he should count himself lucky.

Before his father had died, he, Owen, and Jack had been constantly treading the line between propriety and scandal. He had caused more than one lady's father to eye him askance during a house party or a ball. Leo openly admitted he loved pleasure and the challenge of wooing a woman into his bed. But those days were gone. He was supposed to be keeping out of trouble to restore the family name. The last thing he needed was his mother getting into more trouble than usual.

The dowager countess perched regally, and one hand brushed a few loose hairs back into her elaborate coiffure. The light threading of silver amidst the gold was the only hint of her middling years having just passed. Considering how unhappy her marriage had been to his father, it was impressive that she still looked so well. It never ceased to upset him to think his father had spent nights in the arms of another when he had a beautiful wife at home. But then again, his father had been quite a fool.

"We are finally out of our year of mourning, and I wish to *enjoy* life." Her words were wistful in a way that made his chest tight. Her eyes narrowed as she continued. "I wasn't allowed to do so while the old tyrant still lived." The biting edge to her tone made him wince.

He had known his parents suffered through a loveless marriage, but her frankness about it was a little unsettling. One was not supposed to talk of such things so openly, but his mother had always been open. She was wild where his father had been cold and calm. He'd taken after her in that regard, and she'd never once challenged him on his rakish ways or his tendency to break the hearts of young ladies. But that was because he was a man; a lady had a higher duty to herself and to society to avoid scandal. If his mother was talking of living recklessly, he did not want to know the details. Leo dreaded whatever scheme she was planning now that she could enter society again without violating the strict dictates of her mourning period.

"Well?" She lifted a teacup to her lips, sipping it patiently.

"Well what?" He drank his water and studied her over the rim of the crystal glass. Since his father had died, he'd grown closer to his mother and he'd learned to read her. Right now, she was waiting for him to make the first move in this game she was playing.

For the last few months she'd been working tirelessly to get him away from Hampton House and to return to London. He knew he should be suspicious of her schemes but he wasn't going to fall back into old habits, no matter how tempting it would be to call upon his friends, spend nights at his club, live the life of a wild bachelor as he'd done well enough before his father died. Things were different now.

I cannot be that man anymore, the carefree fool who didn't know his life was on the brink of collapse.

His father's passing had left a hefty amount of death taxes that could bankrupt Hampton, and it was Leo's duty to find a way out from under that crushing weight. After the last three days in London and his continued failures to find a source of additional income, he was afraid for the future of his family. His estate wasn't the only one in danger of being broken by debts.

Only last week he'd visited the neighboring property to the west and learned that the Ashfords were selling their house because Lord Ashford's death had left them deeply in debt. An auctioneer had been examining family portraits and the collection of china and silver while Lady Ashford wept quietly in the corner of the drawing room, her two children sitting beside her, faces drawn tight with grief. It was a bloody bleak affair and Leo would not let that happen to Hampton. Even if it meant sacrificing his own happiness, he would see the estate remain intact.

His mother cleared her throat when he failed to respond. "Let's hear your objections. I know you wish to stop me and will insist we both live frugally and quietly."

Those very words had been on the tip of his tongue. He was a man of business and was keeping the Hampton estate alive based on such notions. Still...he preferred not to face his mother's obvious scorn over the valuable life lesson his father's passing had taught him. To care for a vast estate, a man could not simply gallivant about and live like a veritable rogue as he had when he'd been younger. It was even more important that he work to clear the Hampton name in society or they would be in dire straits before long. His father's mistress and the unsavory way he'd passed in her bed had set tongues wagging and doors slamming in his face so hard that Leo was afraid he might never be viewed reputably.

His days of wildness were behind him. He had his duty to his lands and to his family. They could not let this house be sold or their lives destroyed by losing a home that had been his family's for three hundred years.

"What"—he paused, hoping his concern didn't show—"exactly do you intend to do by indulging in scandalous behavior?" It was entirely possible that his mother's idea of scandal was far tamer than his. They were called the gentler sex for a reason.

"I am going into the village to attend a little political meeting. I've arranged to meet some ladies who share my views and—"

"Good God! You aren't talking about that women's suffrage nonsense, are you?" Leo set his napkin on the table and scowled imperiously at his mother.

Mina's brows arched and her spine stiffened. "I most certainly am. I am quite moved by their cause. Did you know we once had the right to vote? Back in the days of feudal society?"

Leo groaned and nearly smacked his palm into his forehead in frustration. God's teeth, this was not a matter he wished to be dealing with.

"Mother, you cannot go to any such meeting, and I don't give a bloody damn if women were voting back in the days of mud and squalor. That was the damned middle ages for Christ's sake. People were dropping dead of plague and nothing in life was certain. Now things are safe; there's no need for women to have a vote. The men of this country are quite capable of deciding matters of state for you."

The stark look of pain and rage in his mother's eyes was startling. He hadn't expected to see her react so... openly to his words.

"How can you say that...to *me*? After the way your

father made us live, you would continue to deprive me of a voice?"

Leo rubbed his temples. "*No*, that's not what I meant, Mother. Please, try to understand. I have much to do and I cannot be worrying about you. People in London are talking..." He didn't want to continue but he had to make her understand that her actions could make matters worse.

"Talking? About what?" she asked quietly. Her blue eyes were dark and shadowed now.

"Father, about him and that woman. I couldn't get in to see half the gentlemen I used to before."

His mother seemed to understand now, her blue eyes wide with worry. "It's the money, isn't it? You're worried and we've lost so much face because of...*him*."

His throat tightened painfully and he nodded. He had let her down, had failed to do what he needed to in London, and it was destroying him to see her realize that.

She leaned over and placed one hand on top of his on the table, squeezing it. "Then I shan't go to the meeting. I would like a house party instead. Surely we can afford that?" she asked, hope brimming in her tone.

He smiled a little. "Yes, we can certainly afford a house party, Mother."

She brightened again, the worries chased quickly away. "Excellent! I wish to have it next weekend. Guests will arrive here on Friday and stay through Monday. I'm planning to invite all sorts of people, including Mr. Leighton. He owns the *London News Weekly*, which has all of those sensational articles regarding social and political intrigue. He has a lovely daughter—"

Ahh, therein lies her true goal. Not scandal, but marriage. He almost wondered if her plans to join the ranks of the suffragettes was merely to rile him up. No doubt she assumed he would agree to a house party instead because it was much less scandalous…and it would give her a chance to throw eligible ladies at his feet.

Leo's lips twitched. She was clever, his mother, but not clever enough to fool him into putting himself up for sale on the marriage mart. He waved a hand in the air.

"No. No matchmaking. You know full well that I intend to propose to Mildred Pepperwirth." He had been planning this for the last two months. He'd been to see their neighbors in Pepperwirth Vale and had made his intentions to Viscount Pepperwirth quite clear. Mildred was a good, solid choice for a wife. Beautiful, intelligent, and with a clean established English pedigree that would raise the Hampton title back up in the eyes of society.

An extremely unladylike snort escaped his mother's lips. "Bah! Mildred Pepperwirth. Leo, dear, are you determined to give me dull, witless grandchildren? Don't repeat my mistakes." Her eyes darkened and the lines around her eyes and mouth seemed more pronounced as she frowned. "Marry for love. Marry a woman who makes you furious, who drives you mad, a woman who makes your heart bleed if you even think of living one day without her. Don't marry some simpering fool with a hefty dowry simply because you feel compelled to do your duty to your father and this house. She isn't the woman for you. You need someone forward thinking, dear, and Mildred...well...She is far too traditional."

"Traditional is exactly what I need, Mother. You'd have me marry some suffragette who'd tear down the laws and rules that keep our society intact? It would destroy my estate." How the devil had his mother circled back to the topic he wished for her to forget?

"I think those women who fight for the vote are wonderful!" His mother's voice rose a little and color deepened her cheeks. If he wasn't careful, he'd upset her again and he didn't want to do that. *Best to concede some battles in order to win the war, as Owen Hadley would say.* Owen would know, of course, seeing as how he'd fought in the war where battles had been all too real.

"They are indeed brave ladies, Mother. I wouldn't disagree on that. I simply think they would not make the most respectable of wives. I need someone I can depend upon to support my decisions for the estate, not undermine them." A woman with her head in the clouds, dreaming of voting and equal rights was...trouble. He could admire a woman for fighting for something she believed in, but he certainly didn't want to marry a woman like that.

"You'd doom yourself to a life without love?" Her voice trembled slightly as though she were deeply wounded by his reaction. She made as if to stand, but he reached out, caught her hand, and held it.

"Mother, sit. *Please.*" Her words stirred something in him, and he wasn't sure if he liked the idea...to get so lost in another person that you could not live without them. His father had done that with his mistress, a woman who hadn't cared for him the moment she knew her furnished lifestyle was at an end. Leo wanted to avoid such a fate with every fiber of his being.

Living a reckless bachelor life was one thing, but he'd never been foolish enough to allow himself to fall in love. It would be far too dangerous to open one's self up to such a weakness. He didn't want anyone to have power over his heart. His mother had loved his father, and she'd ended up perfectly unhappy when he'd abandoned her for a mistress. Love was a risk he would not take. He shoved the idea out of his mind, focusing on things he knew he could control.

"I think a house party is a wonderful idea, Mother. But do invite some people *I* know. I saw Hadley at the club yesterday. Drop him an invitation for me. In fact, invite the Pepperwirths as well." He winked at her. She rolled her eyes and sighed dramatically. He swore she muttered something about Mildred under her breath. Leo stifled a laugh. As long as his mother was in a mood to fence with him verbally, that meant she was all right and he hadn't upset her too terribly by refusing to let her attend the suffragette meeting.

He wasn't thrilled about the social obligations that houseguests would create, but he couldn't deny he had been burdened lately with far too much work. A party might improve his mood if only for the distraction it would provide. It was a pity he was no longer able to indulge in old habits. The Leo Graham he'd once been would have made it his mission to bed every willing and lovely lady under his roof.

Damn being respectable. It was going to kill him.

I'll have to find some other means of entertainment.

Keeping his mother from marrying him off to someone during the party would be his chief objective, and it would be amusing to see what schemes she came up with.

"You really insist I invite the Pepperwirths?"

He nodded, biting his lip to hide a smile as he enjoyed her squirming. He knew she liked Lord and Lady Pepperwirth, but she balked at his idea of marrying Mildred, simply because she found Mildred boring.

His mother threw up her hands and huffed. "Leo, shame on you. I expected more of a reaction than that. How is it you're a child of *my* blood?"

She stood to leave, and he could only sit back in his chair and glance down at Ladybird. Her canine brown eyes met his, and she seemed just as perplexed as he was by the entire situation. Her tail thumped the ground rhythmically and she nudged his hand until he stroked her head.

His mother wanted him to run off with a woman who made his blood burn. He couldn't afford to. Hampton needed its earl to be calm and in control. Many of his peers were not adjusting to the new age and thus were losing everything their families had built over centuries. His mother was too old-fashioned to see the changes sweeping England. Farmland was less valuable, and the tenancies on the estate weren't prospering as they had in the past.

Leo couldn't even begin to count the hours he'd spent working until the last candle burned out in his study. Or the endless meetings he'd arranged with his steward, Mr. Holmesbury, as they tried to salvage what they could of a crumbling way of life. *Their way of life.* Everything that mattered to him. They could lose it all if he didn't succeed. Grand houses cost far too much, as did the servants they employed.

Running the tip of his finger over the white china plates fringed with a blue flower pattern, he drew in a deep breath. A heavy weight settled over his chest and shoulders, an invisible burden he could not remove, not so long as he continued to love Hampton House and the people who lived within it. They were a part of this place, a part of its history, just as he was.

If any sacrifices could be made, he would fight to keep Hampton just as it was for as long as possible. He had made his plans. He would marry Mildred, use her fortune to sustain Hampton during the transitions taking place in England, and that would be the end of it. Nothing would change his mind. *Nothing*.

Wilhelmina, Dowager Countess of Hampton, peered around the door to the dining room, watching her son finish his luncheon in silence. Ever since he'd returned from London a week ago, he'd been glum and predictable in his daily routine. Working from morning till midnight.

Leo took another bite of his lunch before he reached for the stack of letters on the silver tray to his left, a soft sigh escaping as his shoulders drooped. Ladybird sat at his side, tail swiping across the floor in gentle swishes as she waited for crumbs. The dog whined softly and he petted her absently.

He painted a perfectly boring picture of country life, and it deepened the ache in her heart for him. Leo had been a wonderful child, always exploring, always questing for adventures and causing trouble, the way any good lad should. Mina hadn't been deaf to the rumors of his many paramours or the broken hearts he'd left behind him. At least he'd been a man of passion and action.

Now he was...not. This new Leo was not a son she wished to call her own. He was world-weary, his eyes dark with sorrow and his lips perpetually pursed as he let worries and anxieties drown him. How could he not see that only the bold and courageous men would continue on in this new world, where the ancient houses were crumbling and being broken apart?

She shuddered. The Ashfords had heard their home would be gutted and the grand staircases, the tapestries, even the marble tiles would be sold off to different bidders. Nothing would be left of the grand house or the family who had lived there nearly as long as the Grahams had lived at Hampton House.

We are soon to be ghosts of a forgotten era. We must change; we must adapt. It was one of the reasons she was so determined to attend the suffragette meeting in the small village close to Hampton House. A good number of ladies were coming down from London to attend in order to escape the harsh reactions their gathering would draw in London. Things had to change; *people* had to change. Men needed to recognize that women were just as smart and as valuable in society.

Leo could not marry a traditional woman. He needed

someone who would stand at his side and face the future without fear. Mina would do just about anything to see him married to a fierce Amazon who would battle at his side.

"My lady?" Mr. Gordon, the butler, whispered as he joined his mistress by the door.

She turned and placed a finger to her lips and pointed to Leo.

"Have all the preparations been made for our guests?"

Gordon's face, usually a study of seriousness, softened with pride, and he puffed his chest a bit. "Of course, my lady. I received a telegram from Mr. Leighton. Miss Ivy is coming down early in her father's motorcar."

Mina moved back a few steps from the door as she clapped her hands together in silent glee. Her plan was coming together perfectly. She'd invited Ivy down to Hampton on the pretext of attending the suffragette meeting together, and she'd convinced the young lady that visiting for the house party would be fun.

"Did Mr. Leighton say if he was able to tamper with the motorcar?"

Gordon frowned a little, concern darkening his expression as he handed her the folded telegram. He had known Miss Ivy as long as Mina had and the idea of putting her at risk seemed to upset him.

"Mr. Leighton assured me her motorcar would be close enough to the house but that she'd be stranded. We should make sure to suggest his lordship take a drive around half-past two on Friday. He'll be sure to come across her on the main road."

She hastily read the note herself, grinning a little before slipping it into her dress pocket.

Poor Leo. He was most determined to marry that awful Pepperwirth girl. If all went according to Mina's plans, his intended betrothal would soon be at an end, and her son would fall in love with a woman far more worthy of him. A girl he'd known many years ago, one who'd loved him with all her heart before tragedy had forced their destinies apart.

Ivy Leighton was a modern woman who shared Mina's views on women's rights and would be the best match for her son. Assuming he could see past the fact that she was a suffragette. Mina's lips twitched. No doubt when he met Ivy again, he would find her very grown up and very much changed from the little girl who used to stare at him with stars in her eyes and her heart on her sleeve. She only hoped he would see Ivy as Mina did, as the woman who could save his soul and save Hampton House.

Perhaps I am a meddlesome mama, but Leo should know that I won't leave his choice of wife up to fate.

Chapter 3

Ivy Leighton swiped at the billowing black clouds smothering her. Coughing, she removed her driving goggles and tossed them onto the seat of her new Hudson Speedabout. The *broken* speedabout. Her father was going to be furious. She'd asked to drive it, and only a few miles from her destination, the engine had made a ghastly screeching sound like a dying falcon. Dark smoke plumed out from beneath the yellow hood, painting a dark picture against the deep blue sky.

"Oh dear," she groaned.

She wiped her brow with the back of a gloved hand and it came away dirty. A cool September breeze teased at a loose tendril of her hair from beneath her flat hat. She tried to brush it away, but the thick veil tied around her hat made it more than a little complicated. She unbuttoned her tan linen duster, feeling a little flustered by the Hudson's sudden failure.

What on earth was she going to do? Walk to Hampton House? Why had she thought coming early by herself was a good idea? Because she was plagued by curiosity. Sixteen years ago she had left Hampton, her mother's body barely cold in the ground. How much had the place changed? How much had *he* changed?

Leo...his name still made her shiver.

Handsome, charming Leo. When she'd been eight, he'd been sixteen, and a lifetime seemed to have separated them. Now she was twenty-four and he had to be...she did the math. Thirty-two? Would he still have the ability to consume her soul with those fathomless blue eyes? A part of her was afraid to see him again after all these years. Had her girlhood memories been the stuff of fantasies or was he still the man she'd always loved?

After six Seasons in London, she hadn't found anyone who measured up to Leo Graham, the Earl of Hampton, and she feared she never would. But...what if she arrived at Hampton House and found that he wasn't the man she believed him to be?

With a little shake of her head, Ivy recalled the way he used to tease her, tap the tip of her nose with a finger and call her Button.

"Button indeed," she muttered.

Her nose was no longer buttonlike, at least not

completely. Leo hadn't seen her since she'd outgrown her oversized eyes, knobby knees, and pert nose. Ivy tried to quell the fleet of butterflies that stormed against the battlements of her stomach.

She was nothing like the English beauties who were so favored by the gentlemen at the balls during the Season. That was the problem with being half Gypsy rather than a full-blooded English rose. Still, she knew she was pretty, in an exotic sort of way, but would Leo think her desirable? Ivy had been a favorite of many men. Her father's position, as well as her own heritage, made them believe she had no morals.

A non-Romani or *gadjo's* sense of Gypsies was always wrong. Women of the Romani culture were anything but loose. Still, that awful cultural misunderstanding led to more than one man to offer her a position as his mistress. An offer that she had to politely refuse without making a scene, even though such a request deserved a slap.

Hopefully Leo would be different.

Not that I should truly care, she reminded herself. She was only coming to Hampton House to see the dowager countess and to attend a suffragette meeting with her. Lady Hampton had insisted that Ivy stay for the house party. She'd reminded Leo's mother that she wasn't coming to husband hunt but to see old friends. Ivy firmly believed a modern woman couldn't have a husband, at least not a man born into the British peerage. They stood against women's rights and that was something that she could never reconcile.

She'd watched her mother work tirelessly as a servant for years in a world where her voice hadn't mattered. Witnessing her mother's inability to live the life she truly wanted before she'd died had changed Ivy. Without the right and the power to speak, a person ceased to exist.

After her mother died, she'd been reunited with her father and it had become clear just how powerless she was as a woman. Although he loved and adored her, even he could not give her power over her own life in the way men had. She could not even control her own inheritance; it had to be held in trust by a man. It seemed like everywhere she turned was a dead end. No way out. To be ensnared in a gilded cage meant she was still trapped. The thought made her recoil. Marry a man who would trap her and destroy her independence? No, she would never agree to that. But still...seeing Leo again after all this time would be nice.

Turning her attention back to the Hudson, she knew she'd have to leave it on the shoulder of the road for now. As she reached for her valise, the gravel on the road slipped beneath her boots. A panicked cry escaped her lips as she fell headfirst into the space behind the driver's seat. Her legs wiggled in the air as she struggled in vain to propel herself back upright.

"Blast and hell!" she cursed, fighting wildly to get her

body into a position that could leverage her back down. Her dress and coat tangled around her knees.

The purr of another motorcar's engine made her freeze. A cool breeze caressed her where her travel dress bunched around her thighs. Whoever had just stopped on the road had a prime view of her legs.

The motor died. Footsteps crunching on gravel warned her of someone's approach, and her body went rigid in apprehension. Fear ratcheted up inside her until she was gasping for breath and thrashing to get back on her feet.

"Er...excuse me, miss. May I help?" a rich, smooth voice asked.

"Oh, yes, please. I'm in a spot of bother it seems."

"I'm going to touch you, miss. Please do not panic." The man's gloved hands settled on her ankles, then slid to her calves as he pulled her down. Tingles of awareness shot through her body, making her twitch in the oddest places.

Ivy tried not to let it ruffle her that some strange man's hands were on her legs. She'd never liked feeling vulnerable, and this was perhaps the most exposed she'd ever been in her life. It was unsettling to say the least. She slid down the side of the Hudson, her face heating and the blood pounding in her ears. When she turned to her rescuer, her heart skittered to a stop, and she sucked in a breath.

Leo.

For a long moment she couldn't think, couldn't

breathe. She was a girl again, crying as her mother lay dying. Leo's long, muscular body had been solid and warm behind her as he held her while she wept. He'd been comfort and heat and light where she'd only endured darkness in her mother's last hours.

Of course it would be *him*. He'd be the one to find her covered in road dust, legs flailing in the air, and stuck with a broken down motorcar. She was always at her worst when he was around. Lady Fate evidently didn't like her.

Is there no end to my bad luck?

"Thank you," she said, uncertain if she should say her name. Would he even remember her? Surely not...

With an unexpected deftness, he adjusted her hat, which had been knocked slightly askew during her tumble into the motorcar, and pushed the sides of the veil back as though to get a better look at her face. His lips kicked into a grin, and her heart fluttered back to life. Lord, the man was handsome. His aquiline nose and strong jaw, lips a little thin, but no less appealing, and a halo of golden hair blowing in the breeze. And those eyes, eyes she'd dreamt about for years. More beautiful than she'd remembered.

"You're welcome, Miss..." He waited for her to introduce herself.

So he didn't remember her, then? It stung, yet perhaps that was for the best, given the secret mission Leo's mother had entrusted her with. It was best he did not recognize her and she did not wish to be remembered as "Button."

"My name is Ivy Leighton."

Her name had no effect on him, not that it should have. She'd taken her father's surname after she'd left Hampton and she couldn't remember a time when Leo had called her Ivy. Perhaps he didn't even know it was her name. She hadn't mentioned her mother's maiden name, Jameson, so there was the real possibility he wouldn't recognize her at all. Ivy wasn't a unique name, not really.

Leo captured one of her gloved hands and pressed a kiss to her knuckles. "It's a pleasure to meet you, Miss Leighton, even under such trying circumstances." His lips twitched at the last few words as though he was doing his best not to tease her. "I see you are having some difficulties with your automobile." His eyes roved over the state of the smoking motorcar behind her, assessing the situation.

She tilted her head to the side. Something was different about him, and it wasn't simply that he'd grown into a man and left the last traces of his boyhood behind. No...he had changed, and she couldn't put her finger on how. There was a seriousness to him, a grave solemnity of a man who'd suffered tragedy and loss and now bore a heavy burden. It gave her a bittersweet longing for the young man he'd once been and a respect for the man he'd become now. One thing that had not changed was the effect of his devastating smile. He could have made a fortune bottling it and selling it to lonely hearts throughout England.

In his unbuttoned Burberry motoring coat, trousers, and cap, Leo looked every inch a man of leisure. Yet a silver pocket watch chain glinting in the sunlight lent him an air of authority and precision. An altogether different impression from the boy he'd once been who'd spent an evening capturing glow worms with her in the garden or comforting her after she'd had a rough day and scraped her knee while running about.

She remembered grinning at him so broadly her cheeks hurt as he bent down to show her a captured insect between his palms. The green light had illuminated his face as he studied the black insect. In that moment, they'd been bound together by a spell of twilight and an effervescent glow. Having to stay still, breaths held, so as not to frighten the shy glowworm into darkening her shine. Her heart clenched in longing for warm summer nights like those again. She swallowed the sudden sense of homesickness for a place she'd forced herself to try and forget.

"It was very kind of you to stop and help a lady in distress." She offered a smile, hoping the action would lift her spirits. She had to put memories of that sixteen-year-old boy with merry, twinkling eyes and a tempting smile behind her or she'd be lost. *He's not for you; you cannot fall in love with him, not again.* The Leo she faced now was businesslike and polite, with only a hint of that charming, troublemaking boy she remembered so well.

What had changed him? Had his mother been right that his father's death and the pressures of running the estate had turned him cool and passionless? She'd heard some of the rumors about his father but wasn't sure if they were true. Given how the whispers of his father's mistress had persisted, it had likely affected his reception with most of the respectable families in the city. Even now she could see a hint of that resigned expression in his beautiful eyes. Where was the fiery young man who'd stolen her heart? *No wonder Lady Hampton begged me to come visit him.*

"I'm sorry, I haven't introduced myself. I am the Earl of Hampton. I would be delighted to help, though I confess to knowing nothing of motorcar engines. If you permit, I shall escort you to your destination and send my mechanic to repair your automobile and return it to you." As Leo spoke, he leaned in, placing one hand against the car beside her hip, and she shivered at the scent of him and his warmth. She had always been aware of him; like a planet hugging a distant star, she was connected to him in ways she'd never been with any other man. And that was what made him so dangerous to her. He was perhaps the one man in all of England who could tempt her into falling in love. And love would ruin all of her dreams for a brighter future as a woman with rights. Still, she had promised Lady Hampton she would visit the house and see Leo; she simply needed to guard her heart while she was here.

"My lord, it seems we are both fortunate. My destination is in fact Hampton House. I was invited by the countess for her house party."

This caught him by surprise. His eyes narrowed slightly as his gaze swept her body. Within her tan duster covered in dirt, Ivy must have looked a fright. Not that she could have helped her appearance, but she would have loved to have met him again under better circumstances.

Comprehension showed in the widening of his eyes as he made some mental connection. "My mother invited you? You aren't the newspaper fellow's daughter, are you?"

The newspaper fellow? So Lady Hampton had mentioned her coming, then. Over tea, Lady Hampton had outlined a scheme to play a game upon Leo that required some level of discretion as to Ivy's identity. Leo's mother was convinced he would be too well behaved if he realized Ivy had once been the child he'd looked after. It would be better to hide her identity for a time so she could be treated like any other lady he might meet. The idea of deception hadn't set well with Ivy, but she had to admit she did not want him thinking of Button during the house party.

I'll tell him who I really am, after he has a chance to know me as a woman.

"My father is indeed the newspaperman." She chuckled. He wasn't the first to react that way to her father's background. Leo's eyes were still fixed upon her face and she tried not to wriggle under the intense scrutiny of his gaze. It made her feel warm in the oddest places, and it was much more like the Leo she'd known as a girl.

"Fortunate indeed that I found you, then." He looked over her shoulder into the motorcar. "Your luggage?"

Before she could step out of the way, he moved, accidentally pressing her against the door. A flush of heat coursed through her in a sudden rush when he didn't immediately step back. His eyes blazed with an unexpected interest that made her feel small and vulnerable. As though he could see through her, pick apart her soul, and study the pieces and understand her. What a terrifying thought...Never had she wanted a man to evoke such a feeling, but with him, it was exciting, rather than frightening. Ivy licked her lips and his eyes tracked the movements the way a lion would a mouse.

"Your"—he breathed deeply—"bag," he murmured, sliding past her to reach into the Hudson. He retrieved it without any of the trouble she'd had. "This way."

He gestured toward his auto, which was parked next to hers.

It was a lovely black Stanley Touring motorcar. Her

father had almost bought the same model instead of the Hudson, but in the end he'd opted for the striking yellow auto, valuing the flash more than the extra seats.

Leo walked ahead of her, placing her luggage behind the front passenger seat.

Ivy retrieved her eye goggles and hastily got into her side of the Stanley, which earned her a raised brow by Leo, who had only just turned to try and open the door for her. For some reason, she needed a moment of space between them, at least long enough to get her breath and her good sense back. How was a woman supposed to concentrate around such an irresistible man? When he was too close, she seemed to think only of him and wonder if his lips were as soft as they looked.

Once they were driving back down the road, he turned to look at her.

"Are you traveling alone? Mother mentioned your father was coming. I'm sure she would have insisted you be escorted." There was a note of disapproval to his voice that she didn't like.

She hesitated before replying. "My father is coming tomorrow afternoon on the train, and he's bringing my lady's maid and his valet. Your mother said one of her upstairs maids could wait upon me until they arrived."

"So was that your father's Hudson?"

The question prickled her because his tone seemed to imply a woman could not own a motorcar. It was her father's but only because she insisted they share a vehicle, when he offered to buy her one of her own. They didn't need two; that would have been silly.

"It is," she replied a tad stiffly. "But I have plenty of experience driving it."

Let him think what he will about that.

Leo was silent for a moment. "So...you are...friends with my mother?"

Ivy nibbled her bottom lip, considering how best to answer that. Lady Hampton had always looked out for her as a child, especially when her mother fell ill. The countess was the one who had located Ivy's father and informed him that he had a daughter. For such a service, the word *friend* hardly seemed adequate. Leo's mother was a veritable godsend. But she was supposed to remember the little prank they were to play upon Leo by keeping her real name a secret for a time.

"We met in London three months ago at a charity function held by Lady Buxton." A lie. The countess had crafted a story to explain how they met to keep Leo from discovering Ivy's true identity. She also didn't want Leo knowing that she and Ivy were involved in the Women's Social and Political Union together. When Ivy had questioned the deceptive plan, Lady Hampton had explained her predicament vaguely, saying Leo had become too rigid, too driven, and wasn't open in his thinking, especially toward the suffragette movement.

"He needs adventure and mystery, my dear, and you can provide both. It shall be a fun game. He needs to be shocked for his own good."

But Ivy had grown up at Hampton House and worried the servants would recognize her. The countess had insisted that the servants who'd known her as a child had been instructed to treat her as they would any guest, not as the child they had helped raise.

Ivy had no desire for "Button" to be resurrected in Leo's mind, and a few days of simply being herself would be fun. She would not play the deceiver long, though. She would tell Leo who she was soon; she would simply leave out his mother's involvement in the local suffragette gathering.

Lost in thought, she didn't immediately realize she was being a poor companion to him. A lady of good breeding would never let herself get lost in thought in the presence of her future host. She glanced at Leo and discovered he was watching her when not checking the road ahead.

"And your father? How did he meet my mother?"

"At the same event. She seemed to enjoy discussing his paper."

Leo's bark of laughter made her frown. "The newspaperman. Mother mentioned he was coming and is quite looking forward to it."

She hoped her father had the good sense to follow the

instructions Lady Hampton gave him and not betray Ivy's true identity by mentioning her mother and Ivy's past at Hampton.

Ivy shivered, now feeling the chill in the air, and rubbed her arms.

"There's a lap rug beneath the seat." His hand bumped into hers as they both reached for it.

"My apologies," he murmured, and withdrew his hand. Ivy's gloved fingers brushed over the blanket. She hastily arranged it over her lap and legs, feeling instantly warmer.

"Thank you, my lord."

He merely nodded. The Stanley rattled and bounced worse than a coach on the road. After a few minutes, Leo spun the wheel and turned onto a gravel drive that stretched toward a massive manor house in the distance.

Hampton.

The vision of it always stole her breath. The tan stones were warm in the September sun and afternoon light glinted off the windowpanes. Fir trees dotted the open grounds in patches like spikes of deep green paint across a lighter emerald canvas. She had forgotten how vast the house was and how beautiful.

Nature blended with the house and the gardens, making it a private world where anything seemed possible. Memories of early morning mists curling around the grounds like milky tendrils stirred within her. She used to chase the peacocks across the lawn with Old John, Leo's old butterscotch-colored cocker spaniel, the dog nipping at the thousand-eyed plumed tail feathers of the ill-tempered birds. Old John had always been called that for as long as she could remember. Had he ever been Young John? She hadn't thought to ask. The silliness of her thoughts made her smile. Hampton had a way of reminding her of being a child again, in small ways that made her heart tighten in her chest. Like dancing rainbows in the library caught from a spinning diamond chandelier, or digging in the cool soil to plant seeds with the ancient gardener, Mr. Matthews.

A little sigh escaped Ivy as she thought of all the hours she'd spent there, the minutes ticking away, never knowing her mother would soon die and she'd lose part of herself forever. Or that she'd lose Hampton forever. Yet here she was, sitting in an automobile with Leo, *coming home.*

About the Author

USA TODAY Bestselling Author Lauren Smith is an Oklahoma attorney by day, who pens adventurous and edgy romance stories by the light of her smart phone flashlight app. She knew she was destined to be a romance writer when she attempted to re-write the entire *Titanic* movie just to save Jack from drowning. Connecting with readers by writing emotionally moving, realistic and sexy romances no matter what time period is her passion. She's won multiple awards in several romance subgenres including: New England Reader's Choice Awards, Greater Detroit BookSeller's Best Awards, and a Semi-Finalist award for the Mary Wollstonecraft Shelley Award.

To connect with Lauren, visit her at:

www.laurensmithbooks.com

lauren@Laurensmithbooks.com

facebook.com/LaurenDianaSmith
twitter.com/LSmithAuthor
instagram.com/Laurensmithbooks

Made in the USA
Columbia, SC
09 December 2023

28079745R00157